Victoria Pade

THE CASE OF THE MAYBE BABIES

Harlequin Books

TORONTO • NEW YORK • LONDON
AMSTERDAM • PARIS • SYDNEY • HAMBURG
STOCKHOLM • ATHENS • TOKYO • MILAN
MADRID • WARSAW • BUDAPEST • AUCKLAND

ISBN 0-373-16590-0

THE CASE OF THE MAYBE BABIES

Copyright © 1995 by Victoria Pade.

Printed in U.S.A.

Chapter One

"Here we go," Lindsey Strummel told her own reflection in her car's rearview mirror.

She was parked at the curb in front of the two-story redbrick house she'd grown up in. The house that now belonged to her oldest brother—Quinn—and was also the sight of the offices of Strummel Investigations, the private-detective agency in which she and Quinn shared a partnership.

Inside the house Quinn, his fiancée Cara, Cara's grandmother, and Logan—the Strummel middle child—were celebrating Quinn's and Cara's engagement. But Lindsey had left the party early to meet with a prospective client. Her first in three months.

"You can do this," she said like a cheerleader, finger-combing the full bangs of her short, waifishly styled dark brown hair with its close-cropped sides and back, and full, fluffy top.

But her cheeks were a little pale in spite of the pep talk.

She'd been eager to take on a case of her own again. She just hadn't imagined that it would have anything to do with kids.

Babies, actually.

And that was the rub.

She pinched her cheeks, hoping to put some color into them, and then realized her lips had disappeared into the pallor, too.

She dug a tube of gloss out of her purse and applied it, noticing for the first time that her eyes were open so wide she had the look of a doe caught in headlights.

But that made her laugh at herself.

"Now, don't be dumb," she said impatiently.

In her three and a half years as a private investigator she'd faced down deadbeat dads angry for being located, two-hundred-pound hulks being served summonses, even the barrel of a gun or two.

In view of the numerous times she'd been in real danger, how could just the prospect of taking on a case that involved the younger set knock her off her pins?

Especially when it wasn't uncommon for her to deal with issues having to do with children. They'd been her stock-in-trade as a social worker. And she'd had any number of cases since becoming a P.I. that had had something or other to do with them.

But the point was she'd wanted to get back to work so she could reconnect with the world of adults. So she could stop thinking about kids. And motherhood. And Bobby.

This deal was not what she'd had in mind.

Maybe she should go inside and tell Quinn he'd have to take this one, that she'd wait for the next—like a relay racer with a rock in her shoe. . . .

But the idea of admitting to her brother that she wasn't up to the job was an even worse proposition than facing the job herself.

"Nooo. You can do this," she cajoled, adjusting the mirror for driving and settling back in the seat.

She took a deep breath and held it for a moment as if it would give her strength, and when she blew it out she started the engine and made a fast U-turn to head for the highway.

Good. It felt good to be on the go again. To have a purpose.

"Graham Dunn, here I come," she said as she merged into highway traffic aimed for Evergreen, a small community that eased its way into the mountains.

With renewed determination she forced her thoughts into a work mode by reviewing in her mind her brief phone conversation with the potential client—he of the deep, masculine, sexy voice.

Although she didn't know why it was that she'd noticed such a thing.

He'd come home from an early-morning jog today to find twins sitting in the middle of his bedroom floor. One boy. One girl.

He didn't know where they'd come from. Who they were. How they'd gotten there. Why they'd been left. Or by whom.

And he needed someone to find out.

As Lindsey drove she began to make mental notes of the questions she would need to ask. The course the investigation would have to take if Graham Dunn was on the up-and-up and she accepted his case. And the more the wheels of her mind began to turn, the better she felt. The higher her confidence grew. The greater her sense that she'd made the right decision about returning to work.

She really could do this.

She straightened in her seat, raised her small chin, took another deep breath and blew it out.

She'd be just fine.

Just fine.

Lindsey Strummel was back in the saddle again.

WHATEVER GRAHAM DUNN did for a living, he did it well, Lindsey thought a half hour later when she passed through Evergreen's business-and-shopping district and wound her way through an area of large homes, each set on what she guessed to be about two acres of prime mountain property.

Following her potential client's directions, she found his place, a sprawling ranch-style house built of unrefined stone and no small share of windows. It sat halfway up a steep hillside within a horseshoe of huge spruce trees, partially obscured in front by several stands of aspens.

Before turning up the road that led to the house, Lindsey stopped her car to take a good look around.

The smell of pine trees, loamy soil and woods scented the air like a Christmas potpourri. Even though Denver was still enjoying summer weather, at this altitude autumn was creeping in and the aspen leaves were already gilded bright gold. All in all it was a gorgeous setting. Clean air, no mean streets, peace and quiet.

Whoever had abandoned their kids had picked a nice spot.

If there was such a thing as a nice spot to abandon kids.

Lindsey took note of the fact that there was no wall marking the perimeter of Graham Dunn's lot, no security gates blocking the drive up to his house. Nothing that would inhibit intruders. Or someone playing stork.

There were three other houses she could see from where she was, but all of them were great distances from one another and nestled in their own havens of privacy. It seemed unlikely that anybody inside one of them had seen or heard much of the comings and goings at their neighbor's house. If, indeed, there were people inside them, for there were no signs of life or cars parked anywhere, and Lindsey realized that in spite of the size and high real-estate value, it was possible they were vacation homes or weekend retreats.

She finally turned up the road, not envying Graham Dunn the climb after a winter storm. But on this mid-September day, the pavement was dry and she had no problem reaching that portion of the mountain that had been leveled for his home.

A brick driveway ran straight back to a separate three-car garage, but she didn't go that far, parking just over the crest as soon as all her wheels were on flat ground.

She turned off the engine and got out but again she paused to have a look around.

She couldn't see any of the other three houses from there, so she nixed the notion that the baby drop had been witnessed and decided knocking on doors would be a waste of time.

Then she headed for the house, following a slate-tiled path that meandered through the aspens and landscaping, which was so well done that the minor refinements of artfully planted wildflowers and moss-covered rocks only enhanced the forest floor.

Between that fact and the house itself, which managed to be elegant and rustic at the same time, blending in with its surroundings almost as if it had sprouted there on its own, Lindsey began to form an image of

Graham Dunn as a man more concerned with the natural order of things than with showing off.

If, indeed, it had been his doing and not that of a wife he just hadn't mentioned in their brief talk on the phone this morning.

Two stairs took Lindsey up to the front porch, and as she crossed it to a large carved-oak door she heard a baby's wail from deep inside the house. Just that was enough to make her stomach tighten into a knot.

But she pushed down the urge to run the other way and rang the doorbell with a quick jab of her index finger, as if that committed her.

She heard heavy footsteps just before the door opened—with a certain amount of desperation and force behind it. And there stood a tall, powerfully built man who looked as if he'd just been in a food fight. And lost.

"Mr. Dunn?"

"Yes?" he answered a little impatiently, frowning at her in a way that creased a strong forehead and at the same time narrowing eyes that were electric blue and very disarming both in their unusual color and the penetrating way in which he stabbed her with them.

"I'm Lindsey Strummel from Strummel Investigations. We spoke earlier today."

The striking eyes widened. "Is it three already?"

"I may be a few minutes early, but it's close."

He looked past her, as if to confirm the time in the slant of the sun, and then stepped out of the way. "Come on in. I'm sorry. I didn't realize it was so late."

Lindsey wasn't exactly sure what he was apologizing for as she went through the door into an entryway as big as her bedroom, separated by a half partition and a step

downward from a living room that most of her house could have fitted into.

A second wail joined the ongoing one and he flinched at the sound. "I'm afraid I'm not doing too well as a baby-sitter. Or a father. Or whatever I am," he said, raising a Paul Bunyan-size hand as if he were going to rake it through his light brown hair. But on the way he seemed to think better of it, glancing at his palm and putting it down again.

Lindsey suddenly had to fight to keep from laughing. It wasn't only his hands that made her think of Paul Bunyan. The man was probably six feet three inches of solid, packed muscle, with the shoulders of an ox. But from the look on his face—his very handsome face—he'd been daunted by his two little surprises.

"I've been trying to get them to eat something," he said.

"Not having a lot of luck?" she guessed, pointing her chin at his food-stained jogging suit.

"No matter what I give them they don't want it."

"That's kids for you."

A loud crash sounded just then, and with only a moment spared to roll his eyes and sigh in frustration, Graham Dunn took off down the hall, which seemed to lead from the entranceway straight into the kitchen at the rear of the house.

And what a mess that kitchen was, Lindsey found when she'd closed the door behind her and trailed him to it.

The wide-open space, which was no doubt ordinarily pristine white with only hints of ice blue in the tiled backsplashes, was splattered with the same variety of foods Graham Dunn wore—spaghetti, scrambled eggs,

some kind of sausages, lunch meat, gravy, jelly and a number of other things that were indistinguishable.

"Caviar," he identified one of them when she stepped through the doorway and over a blob of the tarry stuff.

And there in the midst of the devastation were the two babies, one of them sitting in a serving bowl beside a puddle of soup while the other stood near the glass that had apparently just been thrown against the dishwasher—if the milk that dripped down the front was any indication.

Lindsey guessed them to be fourteen or fifteen months old—slightly past their first birthdays but not all the way to a year and a half.

Their clothes were food-caked, their noses ran down their tiny upper lips, their eyes were red and pouring torrential tears and drool dribbled down their chins.

And Lindsey was drawn to them like a heat-seeking missile.

She grabbed the back of a nearby wicker-and-chrome chair and stayed put, watching as her prospective client surveyed the scene with more of that expression of utter bewilderment.

He pointed to the standing baby and said, "The note says his name is Charlie. The girl is Kate."

And the caterwauling was deafening.

"Have you tried changing their diapers?" Lindsey asked, finding it necessary to raise her voice to be heard over the din.

"I didn't know how," he confessed, sounding embarrassed.

"How about a nap? Have they had one of those?"

"A nap?" he repeated as if that were a novel idea that opened a window of hope for him to escape through. But then he came back down to earth. "I'm afraid I

don't know diddly about babies. Should they have slept since this morning?''

"At least once. Maybe twice."

And it was going to be impossible to talk unless sleeping was exactly what they did now.

But Graham Dunn was hardly likely to whisk them off on his own while she cooled her heels in the clean, sunken living room she'd passed by.

"Look," she said, hating the conclusion she'd come to. "I'll help you clean them up and put them to bed so we can discuss this."

She'd never seen anyone look quite as relieved as he did at that suggestion, whether at the thought of having some peace and quiet, or assistance with the twins, or both.

"I don't suppose we could gently hose them off?" he asked tentatively.

"I think a couple of wet towels would be better," Lindsey instructed.

"I'll get them."

Left alone with the squalling babies, Lindsey silently repeated more of the pep talk that had brought her this far, all the while glancing from one child to the other as if trying to determine which of them might pose less emotional risk to her.

But it was futile, and she knew it by the itch in her arms to scoop them both up.

She finally hunkered down on her heels so she was nearer to eye level with them. But she kept her arms close to her body rather than reaching for them. "It's all right," she said in a soothing voice that was a bit shaky.

That brought a break in the sobbing from both kids as they checked her out.

And then the worst thing that could possibly have happened, happened.

Kate rolled out of the bowl and toddled to her on unsteady legs and a penguinlike gait so flat-footed and wobbly it was clear she hadn't been doing it long.

Apparently that was all Charlie needed to see because he came, too.

And suddenly Lindsey had an arm around each of them as they both took up crying all over again just in case she might have forgotten how miserable they were.

"For a minute it sounded like they were going to stop," Graham Dunn said as he returned with a stack of towels and a large athletic bag.

"Just a breather," she answered, trying to make it sound glib when she felt anything but.

He nodded and set the bag on the nearby glass table. "This was left with them. I guess it has what they need in it."

"What they need right now is to be cleaned up, have their diapers changed and get to sleep," she reiterated when he stood there looking at them as if he'd forgotten. Then she added, "You wet the towels and I'll get them out of these clothes."

That put him into motion. He finally high-stepped over the debris, taking the towels to the kitchen sink.

So, get these kiddos out of their clothes the way you said you would, Lindsey ordered herself, knowing she had to let go of them in order to do it. But knowing it and doing it were two different things. Her arms seemed stuck in place.

Oh, very professional, Strummel, very professional. Latch on to two abandoned kids and freeze. Perfect.

Not wanting to be caught at it, she forced herself to straighten away from the twins and kneeled on the floor, taking her purse from where it hung on her

shoulder and setting it on the seat of the chair she'd anchored herself to before.

Charlie and Kate stood there sobbing even louder, and she knew that wasn't likely to improve when she started undressing them, but that was what she did, anyway.

Luckily they each wore terry-cloth rompers that snapped from throat to ankle so she managed to get them off easily and without smearing food anywhere new. Both kids protested through more tears, but weary arms and legs cooperated heavily in spite of it, letting Lindsey know they were just plain pooped.

About the time she had them free of all but their soggy diapers, Graham Dunn returned with the damp towels.

"This probably won't be nice," she warned. "Kids don't like being wiped up."

He took Charlie by the hand as if the little boy might bite and brought him to stand in front of him where he knelt beside Lindsey. He mimicked exactly what she was doing, as if there was some trick to it.

The only trick was in getting them clean while a cacophony of new wails let it be known they'd rather stay dirty.

And then it was done and out from the blotches of dried food emerged two beautiful babies with eyes nearly as blue as Graham Dunn's, fat rosy cheeks, tiny pink noses and heads full of light brown, downy hair— Charlie having more of it than Kate.

"Diaper changing would be better done on a bed," Lindsey suggested then.

"The guest room," he answered as if she might know where that was.

Lindsey stood, staring at the still-bawling Kate and knowing she should pick her up. *Wanting* to pick her up.

And worrying that once she did she'd never want to put her down again.

But then Kate raised her tear-streaked cherub's face to her and reached out her arms to be held, and Lindsey couldn't do anything less.

Steeling herself, she bent over and scooped up the baby.

And for just an instant it flashed through her mind to run out of that house with her and keep her for herself.

But of course it was only a flash. Nothing she would ever do.

Then she realized Graham Dunn had lifted Charlie, too. But not to neatly tuck him onto his hip, where Kate rode Lindsey's. The big man had the little boy hovering in midair, his giant hands bracketing the tiny ribs just under his arms.

He hadn't been kidding when he said he didn't know diddly about kids. Maybe less than diddly.

"Try it like this," Lindsey suggested, showing how she had Kate situated.

There was some initial clumsiness but her potential client finally managed to copy the position, and while Kate still cried, that was all it took for Charlie to stick his middle two fingers in his mouth, lay his head against one of those broad shoulders and finally be quiet.

"Wow," Graham Dunn whispered.

Lindsey just laughed, shook her head and said, "Show me the way to the bedroom."

One of his eyebrows flew up and those great blue eyes suddenly sparkled with mischief before he apparently stopped himself just short of saying what she thought was probably a rejoinder inappropriate for a woman he'd known only a little while. But his recovery was almost seamless and instead he merely said, "This way,"

grabbing the athletic bag to take along and leading her into the hall she'd used before.

Lindsey followed but wondered at herself for feeling the slightest bit titillated at the possibility that she'd inspired something flirtatious in him.

He turned into a connecting hallway and then into a room midway down.

The guest room—like everything else she'd seen of his house so far—was huge and so tastefully decorated in warm browns and beiges, it would make any overnight visitor feel right at home.

She went directly to the double bed where she gently laid Kate on her back. "I'll show you how to change a diaper," she said, expecting him to lay Charlie down, too.

But the man seemed to be enjoying having the little boy curled against his sturdy neck and merely watched from beside her.

Lindsey took the athletic bag from him, opened it and, in the process of pulling out two disposable diapers, discovered a frayed blanket with a satin edge hanging loose from one section like the tail of a kite. "Is this yours, Kate?" she guessed, handing it to the baby, who grasped it like a lifeline. The little girl immediately began rubbing her cheek with that dangling piece of satin and finally stopped her crying, too.

"Amazing," Graham Dunn said when he saw it.

"Poor babies," Lindsey muttered, feeling sorry for how confused and dislocated and disrupted they surely felt.

Her diaper demonstration didn't take any time at all, and Graham Dunn was a quick study, performing the service for Charlie almost without a hitch.

Both babies were heavy lidded when it was over, and since the room was a comfortable temperature Lindsey decided they could be put to bed in only their diapers.

But not before she enlisted her prospective client in pushing the bed against a wall.

"We'll also need to block the other side and the bottom with chairs. These kids are probably used to sleeping in cribs and could roll out."

Again the big man seemed surprised to learn such a simple fact and solution but didn't hesitate to follow instructions.

As he dragged chairs in from the kitchen, Lindsey tucked the twins in. And when they fell asleep almost instantly she told herself to keep her distance. But still she couldn't resist smoothing each tiny forehead with a mother's hand before giving over that last spot at the head of the bed to a chair.

"Whew!" Graham Dunn sighed, sounding exhausted himself.

Lindsey shushed him with a finger to her lips, picked up the athletic bag again and pointed at the door.

When it was pulled closed behind them, he spoke in a low voice. "Would you mind if I take five minutes to change clothes before we talk?"

"No, that's fine. I want to go through the things in this bag, anyway."

"I hadn't opened it before you did, so everything that came with them is still in it. Except the note. I'll bring that when I get back. Make yourself at home."

Lindsey nodded and they went in opposite directions—he to a door across from that of the guest room, and she back into the main hall, heading for the kitchen for her purse.

Even though she was prepared for her second sight of the mess, it was still incredible, and for a moment she was tempted to do some initial cleaning before the food dried. But then she realized that it was bad enough that she'd already had such close contact with the twins, without letting herself stray any further from her role as investigator.

Besides, coming to a man's rescue domestically had already caused her big problems once. It was a mistake she wanted to be careful not to make again.

So rather than touch a single crumb, she merely took her purse and went to the living room in the front of the house.

A stone fireplace dominated one wall and two sofas faced each other across a square box of a coffee table with drawers on all four sides.

She didn't spend the time to inventory the rest of the furnishings because she was too anxious to get on with her work. Instead she merely took her purse and the athletic bag to one of the couches where she sat and unloaded the babies' things one by one onto the coffee table.

It wasn't very enlightening.

The bag held only common things that could have been purchased in any discount store. A half dozen outfits for each child—all clean and folded neatly. Freshly polished shoes—one pair each with the kids' first initials written on the insides to denote whose were whose. Bibs. Diapers. Socks and undershirts. Pajamas. Spring-weight jackets. Winter coats and hats. And at the bottom, a stuffed monkey that was well loved and probably being missed by one of the little imps in the guest room even as they slept.

And that was that. Necessities but no clues.

"Find anything?"

Graham Dunn had come into the room so quietly she hadn't heard him until he spoke, startling her. "No," she answered too brightly, glancing up at him.

The change of clothes had been quick but effective, and for a moment Lindsey was struck by the man's good looks as if seeing him for the first time.

His hair was short on the sides and in back but slightly long on top, just barely falling across his right temple. More than merely handsome, he had an out-doorsy sort of face with a nose that was a bit long, but straight and well shaped, nonetheless. His lips were full but not overly so, his jaw was firm, his chin strong. And faint laugh lines around his oh-so-blue eyes, as well as the deep traces of two creases that ran from the sides of his nose to parenthesize his mouth, all added to the rugged, masculine appearance that would never land him on the cover of *GQ* but no doubt turned heads wherever he went.

Not that it mattered to her, of course. Her appreciation was purely academic. Every bit of it. Even down to being unusually aware of the lithe way he moved across the room and the snug fit of his jeans over hips that were not too narrow, not too wide, and thighs the size of oil drums.

He'd put on a plain white mock-turtleneck shirt, and as he joined her to sit on the facing sofa, he pushed the long sleeves up to his elbows, exposing thick wrists and powerful forearms speckled with hair the same sun-kissed brown color of that on his head.

"Here's the note," he said, using only his index and middle fingers to pull it from his breast pocket to hand it to her. "The kids were on the floor in my bedroom, and that was on the bed where I couldn't miss it."

Glad for the distraction, Lindsey studied the note.

It wasn't much, though.

It was typed on plain white tablet paper and said, *"Congratulations, Graham Dunn, you're a daddy. Say hello to Charlie and Kate."*

Lindsey turned it over and held it up to the light coming in through the picture window that was nearly the whole front wall, but there was nothing else there. No signature. No marks—water or otherwise. No shadows of an indentation from something written on a sheet ahead of it. Nothing. And the fact that it was typed instead of handwritten didn't even leave reason for a guess as to whether the author was male or female.

"How did they gain entry into the house?" she asked, getting the ball rolling as she set the note on the coffee table in front of her and replaced the babies' things in the athletic bag.

"Through the kitchen door in back. There's a glass pane in it and it was broken out. I called an emergency service and had it fixed just before you got here."

"So it was a forced entry. And you don't have an alarm?"

"This is hardly a high-crime area. I never thought it was necessary."

"Was anything taken?"

"No. Or even disturbed. Whoever came in just left the twins and ran."

Lindsey nodded, watching him. He answered her questions with gravity but without melodrama. She liked that.

Not that it mattered whether she liked it or not.

"A break in, abandoned kids... Why didn't you call the police instead of a P.I.?"

He poked his chin toward the note. "I might have except for that." His brow drew in to a frown. "But I figured if I did the babies would probably be taken away, turned over to social services, put in a foster home. And if they're my kids..."

"So there *is* a chance of that."

He closed his eyes, arched his brows and sighed, all as if he found it hard to believe but was afraid to discount the possibility. "I need to know for sure before I just turn them over to red tape, bureaucracy and legalities. If they're my kids, they're my kids, and we don't need to involve criminal authorities."

"And if they aren't your kids?"

"Then I want to know why they're here, what's happening with them, how someone could have done this to them. And once we've discovered all of that I'll want to know what's best for them from here on before I take any kind of action—whether that's returning them or putting them into the system or finding some other place for them."

Good answer. Lindsey liked it. But more than that, she agreed with it.

He went on. "Can we look into all of this without calling in the cops and social workers? Or is that illegal?"

Lindsey wiggled her hand in a so-so gesture. "We're in shady territory, that's for sure. But the note gives us some leeway. If it comes down to notifying authorities we can argue that we thought it was a private matter, that the kids were yours and the mother just dropped them off so you could have a turn at parenthood. I've had enough associations with the police and social services that they won't doubt my word, so we'll be all right doing the investigation on our own for now."

"Does that mean you'll take the case?" He smiled with only one side of his mouth, looking relieved again, but also very charming.

"I guess it does," she answered, tamping down on the tiny embers that seemed to have sparked inside her in answer to that charm.

She cleared her throat and went on with business as if she hadn't noticed it. "Let me get some background information, Mr. Dunn."

"Graham."

"*Graham* Dunn," she repeated as she wrote. "Age?"

"Thirty-six. Yours?"

He said that matter-of-factly, sounding as if he were interviewing her the same way she was interviewing him, so she answered it. "I'm thirty-three. Are you married?" She hadn't seen any signs of a wife or live-in lover, and he hadn't referred to anyone, but she asked, anyway. People—more often men than women—were sometimes talented at presenting themselves as single even when they weren't.

"No, I've never been married. Have you?"

That sounded more conversational but she answered it anyway. Briefly. "I'm recently divorced. Are you currently involved with anyone?" And was that question really relevant?

"No. I'm not even dating anyone right now. Are you?"

She couldn't very well get up in arms about his asking the same thing when she hadn't had a good reason for asking it herself. "No, I'm flying solo for now." Again she didn't elaborate, but she did try putting things on a more impersonal level again by continuing as detachedly as a census taker. "What do you do for a living?"

"I design, manufacture and sell Dunnit Tennis Shoes."

That surprised her, though there was no reason it should have. Clearly he was successful at something, so why not tennis shoes? And Dunnit was one of the most popular brands, rivaling Nike, Adidas and Reebok, and could easily provide for an expensive home in Evergreen.

But somehow it struck her as incongruous with the impressions she'd had of him since meeting him. She might have guessed forest ranger, construction worker, something very physical and outdoorsy. But tennis-shoe designer?

"You hate my shoes?" he guessed when she left too long a silence while she stared at him and tried to realign her preconceived notions.

"No," she said with a laugh at her own mistaken imaginings. "Not at all. I even have a pair. They're great for chasing down people who would rather run than be served a summons. I just didn't picture you as an entrepreneur."

His smile broadened, flashing straight white teeth and lots of them. "What did you picture me as?"

"Paul Bunyan," she admitted before she even realized she was going to, laughing once more at herself.

"I have a drawing table in the other room. And a computer. And even a briefcase if you want to see them," he offered, though clearly without taking offense, more in a teasing vein.

In fact, the air between them suddenly seemed to have taken on a new element altogether—almost as if they'd been on a blind date and had finally clicked enough to relax and enjoy themselves.

Though of course that was an absolutely ridiculous thought. And very unprofessional.

Back to business.

She nodded toward the note on the coffee table. "Congratulations...you're a daddy," she said out loud. "Any idea who the mother is?"

He flinched as if she'd hit him, but comically, this time overtly teasing her. "Paul Bunyan as a womanizer who can't even narrow down the field of who he might have fathered babies by?"

"Paul Bunyan as a monk?" she challenged.

He laughed. "No, not quite. But not a womanizer, either."

"Okay. So go ahead and narrow the field. Down to who you were involved with, say, this time two years ago."

"When the twins were probably conceived."

"Right."

"That field is very narrow. I was in a monogamous relationship then."

And he didn't seem to remember it fondly if his suddenly sober expression meant anything. Nor was he anxious to talk about it because he was certainly not being very forthcoming with the information.

"Have you considered calling the woman and asking if the twins are yours and hers?"

"I considered it."

"But you didn't do it?"

"No. And I'd rather you didn't either, until we have some reason other than the note to believe I might be the father."

Lindsey waited for him to say more. To tell her why he didn't want to take what seemed like the easiest first step—a simple phone call. But he didn't explain.

She decided to try some prompting. "It is possible the twins belong to you and this woman, though?"

He took a deep breath and made a face that resembled a grimace without actually being a full-fledged one. "I used birth control. Conscientiously. But—" he shrugged "—I guess it could have failed."

"So there was no indication she might have been pregnant the last time you saw her?"

"None."

"And when was that?"

"Two years ago. If she was pregnant, she might not have even known it herself. That was right when the relationship ended."

"I'm sorry if this sounds like prying, but . . ."

He smiled at her again. "It's okay. I know you're just doing your job."

"Was the end of the relationship such that she would have kept the news that she was carrying your baby—babies—from you?"

"Yes."

"And not have informed you after they were born, even for financial help?"

"Right."

"In spite of the fact that you could obviously have provided substantially for your own kids?"

"In spite of that."

And he hadn't had to consider his answers because there hadn't been so much as the blink of an eye before he'd given them. Lindsey wondered why.

But then she was beginning to wonder a lot of things.

"If the woman didn't want or need contact with you or assistance from you in the last two years, why do you think she would break a window in your house and dump the twins here now?"

"That's the million-dollar question. I don't have an answer for it."

"Even knowing the woman and the circumstances? You couldn't so much as guess?"

He didn't respond right away. Instead he watched her with those electric blue eyes for a long moment before his sexy mouth stretched into a grin. "Were you a cop before you became a P.I.?"

Okay, so maybe she had begun to sound as if she were interrogating him rather than just gathering background information. But maybe those inappropriate thoughts about how great looking and personable he was had something to do with it.

Or maybe he just didn't want to answer her.

"No, I wasn't a cop before I became a P.I." But she didn't say what she was, either. Two could play this game. "Would you have denied being the father or refused them support had she come to you directly?"

"No. To both of those," he answered just as readily as before and with enough conviction to convince her. "Let's just leave it that I don't know why *anyone* would leave those babies the way they did, but I'm especially confused if they're mine. All it would have taken for me to do whatever I needed to do is to have been told about it."

Once more she studied him, letting silence fall between them. Waiting to see if he would be driven to fill it.

But he only stared back at her. If there was an ounce of guilt in him it didn't show. And if he wasn't telling her the truth he was a better liar than any she'd ever encountered because he lacked the liar's need to elaborate in order to convince her.

No, she believed Graham Dunn was on the level, in spite of whatever he wasn't telling her. And more than that, she couldn't help being just a little impressed by him, too, by the sense she had that he was protecting this woman who might be the mother of his children, even if she had done something as despicable as abandoning them.

And it didn't hurt anything that he was intelligent and charming, that he had a good sense of humor, that he was man enough to face his responsibilities head-on, without a whimper or an excuse. She liked all of that, too.

And maybe before she got to liking much more about him, she ought to leave, she told herself.

She put her notebook back in her purse. "A blood test isn't conclusive proof but it's a good start in lieu of contacting the possible mother. Would you be willing to do that?"

"Absolutely."

"I also think it would be a good idea for the babies to be seen by a doctor. They seem healthy and well cared for, not abused, but just to be sure."

"Good idea."

"I know a pediatrician. I think I can arrange for an appointment tomorrow."

"Great."

"In the meantime I'll check to make sure they haven't been reported missing or kidnapped, and we'll go from there."

She stood and so did he.

"You'll need a retainer, won't you?" he asked.

"It's up to you. I can bill you if you'd rather."

"Are you sure?" he teased again, smiling and deepening the creases around the corners of his eyes and

mouth. "Paul Bunyan might be hard to locate if he takes to the woods."

That made her smile back at him. "I'm a great tracker."

She headed for the front door, but as she stepped into the hallway that stretched to the kitchen at the other end she remembered his ineptitude with the babies and hesitated.

"Do you have a mother or a sister or someone who can come and help you with the twins?" she asked.

"I have a housekeeper but she won't be in until the day after tomorrow," he answered, casting a pained look in the same direction she had.

"How about a neighborhood baby-sitter who could just lend a hand?"

He pointed a long index finger at her. "That's a good idea. There is a girl across the road. I'll bet I can hire her to give me some pointers."

That made Lindsey feel much better. Because until then she'd actually been wondering if she should stay.

"I'd call her while they're still asleep and see if you can get her to help clean up, too," she encouraged as she went out the front door.

Then she looked back at him, standing there smiling at her, with no trace of the harried, frustrated man who'd let her in earlier, and she was amazed to find herself a little jealous of the teenage girl who would come over to take care of those babies and tutor Graham Dunn in parenthood.

And *that* was the craziest thought to have raced through her mind since she'd left Quinn's engagement party that afternoon.

But crazy or not, she knew she'd better get out of there before she actually acted on any misplaced temptation.

"I'll let you know about the doctor's appointment," she told him as she stepped off the porch, finally saying goodbye without really looking at him again.

But when she'd made it all the way into her car she stole a peek at the house and found him outside, one foot on the railing that ran around the porch, his arms braced on his upraised knee, watching her.

And if she still thought of herself as any judge of such things, she might have thought there was more to his expression than just friendliness. More in the way of interest in her as a woman, maybe.

But while she trusted her instincts in other areas, she didn't trust them in regard to anything romantic and she discounted the idea.

Graham Dunn was her client.

Just her client.

And nothing more.

Chapter Two

"Mik."

Graham jolted awake at the sound that came from the guest room, wondered what it had been and then remembered there were actually babies in there. He silently groaned as he squinted his eyes barely open to look at the clock on his bedside table: 5:43 a.m.

Another inward groan.

Why weren't they sleeping? They'd napped until nine the night before and then been awake until four that morning. That was less than two hours ago. How could a full night's sleep be less than a nap?

But there weren't any other noises from across the hall so he closed his eyes again and went on lying there—on his still-made bed, in his clothes, just the way he'd fallen asleep when he'd finally gotten the twins to bed.

Maybe, he thought, *if I'm stone still they'll have mercy on me and go back to sleep.*

"Mik!" came a louder demand.

Milk. By now Graham knew that it was one of the words both kids could say. And that that was Kate's voice. And that when she said it, she meant it. She wanted milk and she wanted it on the double. Or else.

But he was so damn tired. And not only because he hadn't had even two hours' sleep in the last twenty-four. This baby stuff was more exhausting than running marathons. They needed *constant* attention. And when that attention had to come from somebody who didn't know what the hell he was doing, trial and error was a lot more error than anything.

"Mik!"

That was part shout, part whine. The crying would come any minute.

"Lie down and go back to sleep, Kate. It's too early," he called back in a soothing voice, testing to see if it might work.

Ha!

"Mik!" she screamed even louder and more impatiently.

And the sounds that followed told him Charlie was now awake, too.

Oh, God.

Then he remembered that he couldn't leave them in that bed. They would stand and hang on to the backs of the chairs as if they were crib sides, bouncing up and down or rocking back and forth until disaster struck. Charlie already had a knot on his forehead from falling when the chair edged out from under him during one of the eight times Graham had tried to put them to bed for the night.

"Muk."

Yep, that was Charlie, all right. And his variation of the word, delivered in his deeper baby voice.

"I'm coming," Graham said with a weary sigh.

He got off the bed like a ninety-year-old man, feeling as if every muscle in his body had been tensed to the limit while he slept. Stress sleeping. Maybe it could be

a new Olympic event. And he had just the tennis shoes for it—the A-Ps. All-pros. All-purpose. He was still wearing his.

He crossed the hall and flipped on the light, momentarily blinding himself and the kids, too—evidenced by Charlie's "ow" and Kate still rubbing her eyes when Graham's had adjusted and he could see her.

"Sorry, guys," he said, going to them.

They were both standing on the edge of the mattress, four hands grasping the chair backs, watching him as expectantly as if he'd proven himself adept at their care.

"You know, it's too early for us to be up," he informed them, sitting across the two chairs they stood behind.

"Mik," Kate answered reasonably.

"No milk. Sleep." And he sounded like Tarzan addressing Jane.

"Mik?" The bottom lip came out.

Graham sighed and picked her up, sitting her on his lap. "If I get the two of you a drink of milk will you go back to sleep?"

Of course they didn't answer. Instead Charlie rocked back and forth like a monkey against cage bars, wanting to be let out, too.

"Okay," Graham said, trying to sound firm. "A little milk and then it's right back to bed."

He set Kate on the floor and lifted Charlie over the chairs, too. But Kate was not happy to be left to walk while Charlie rode, and Graham ended up carrying them both into the kitchen.

He sat them on the countertop but blocked the edge with his stomach so they wouldn't fall while he did a contortion to take a carton of milk out of the refrigerator.

But the glasses were in a cupboard out of his reach.

In fact, logistics were half the problem with this kid stuff, he thought. Everything was in a different spot than he needed it to be, and his hands were always full of babies.

He looked at them. At the cupboard where the glasses were. At the carton. And he opted for the easiest solution.

"Don't tell anybody we did this," he cautioned, taking a drink directly from the spout to demonstrate. "Open up," he said then, carefully pouring milk into their mouths in the same way.

Of course, like everything he did with them, it made a mess. Kate stopped drinking while he was still pouring, and in the middle of Charlie's turn, the little boy turned his head as if he were drinking from a baby bottle and it would come along. They both ended up with soggy pajamas.

But they'd had milk.

"Can we go back to sleep now?" Graham asked hopefully.

Yet even as he did he knew he couldn't put them in bed wearing wet clothes. So he'd have to change them. Which took forever. And their only other pajamas had already been discarded into a heap on the floor after a peanut-butter-and-jelly snack he'd tried at midnight.

Or he could just take off the pajamas and let them sleep in their diapers the way they had for their nap.

Trouble was, the house wasn't as warm now as it had been then.

"How about we take off the wet things and all lie down together? I'll keep you guys warm that way and maybe we can all get some more rest. What do you say?"

Kate said, "Mik."

He gave her more and then gave Charlie another shot of it, too, just for good measure.

"Okay. Bedtime. Again," he said enthusiastically, putting the carton back in the refrigerator.

Good sign—neither baby cried at the disappearance of the milk.

Graham undressed them there, so his own clothes wouldn't get wet carrying them, and took them back into the guest room.

One after the other he lifted them over the chairs and onto the bed, then he climbed in between them and lay down, holding his arms out so they could lie on either side of him. "Come on."

Kate grabbed her blanket and curled up to him. But Charlie crawled over him, oblivious to the groin injury he nearly caused, and snuggled up against Kate's backside.

Maybe this would actually work.

Graham pulled the bed's quilt over the three of them, relaxed his head on the pillow and closed his eyes, grateful that they seemed to like him enough to cuddle up with him.

Did that mean anything? he wondered.

Was there some instinctive bond that made them sense that he was their father?

But they'd liked Lindsey Strummel just as much, so it probably wasn't an indication.

Then again, he'd liked Lindsey Strummel himself.

And that thought was all it took for his tired mind to conjure up her image when he should have been falling asleep instead.

She was hardly what he'd expected in the way of a private investigator. She was small and wiry, a little dy-

namo he could picture outmaneuvering, outwitting, outrunning the kind of louts she probably encountered in her line of work.

But the face that went with it all had a certain elegance about it that didn't fit the image.

Her skin was as smooth and creamy as alabaster. She had cheekbones high enough for any fashion model. Lips that were so perfect, so soft looking, so sweet that when they'd smiled, his gaze had actually stuck to them a time or two.

Her hair now—that was tomboyish. Short and fluffy and free-falling. But he liked it, anyway. Liked the easy style, the coffee-bean-streaked-with-copper shade. The way it smelled when he'd stood watching her diaper Kate—clean, peachy...

Besides, tomboyish or not, it framed her eyes and they were too stunning not to be accentuated.

Wide, shining silver. He'd never seen eyes quite like that before. So light, so clear, there almost wasn't any color at all. Just a sparkle around black, black pupils. And they came complete with thick, long, sooty lashes that stood out against that porcelain skin like sable against snow.

Beautiful. She really was beautiful. But tempered with a certain earthiness that was very appealing to him.

So appealing, in fact, that he could hardly wait to see her again today....

Whoa! What was he thinking? And was he out of his mind to be thinking it?

Here he was with his hands more full than at any time in his life. In more of a mess, more confusion, more chaos, and he was actually attracted to the person he'd hired to sort through it all?

Not wise.

This was no time for it to happen and certainly not with someone who was going to be looking through the skeletons in his closet.

And yet...

He couldn't help it.

He was attracted to Lindsey Strummel and it was no use denying it.

He just wouldn't do anything about it.

But the disappointment that came with that silent claim was powerful, making him wonder if he really could resist the urge.

Oh, hell, she'd probably do it for him. Who would want a guy with two kids just thrust on him and a past he wasn't proud of? A past she'd no doubt be put off by when she found out about it?

Surely not the lovely Ms. Strummel.

Dammit anyway...

"Mik."

That pulled him from his thoughts, and regrets.

He opened his eyes only enough to look down into Kate's, staring up at him from just above his armpit.

So much for getting any rest.

"Go back to sleep, Kate," he whispered, hoping not to wake Charlie.

But just then Charlie popped up from behind his sister and added his two cents' worth. "Muk."

Graham closed his eyes and blew out a long, resolute sigh.

But there was one good thing about getting up again—the sooner he started this day, the sooner he'd get to see Lindsey again.

And in spite of everything, it was worth it.

IT WAS TEN that morning when Lindsey arrived at the office of Strummel Investigations for work. Like Graham Dunn's driveway, Quinn's ran alongside the house all the way to an old carriage house out back that had been converted into a three-car garage with an apartment on the second level. An apartment that belonged to Logan.

She parked near his door but didn't go up to say good morning the way she sometimes did. She knew he was on duty because she'd called him early that morning to ask a favor, and he'd said he had to be at the police station by eight.

So instead she crossed the yard and went into Quinn's house through the mudroom.

But if Logan had made it to the station, it had been a short day because he was sitting at the kitchen table with Quinn.

"What are you doing here?" she asked in lieu of a greeting to either of her brothers.

But from their somber expressions, she knew Logan's being there wasn't because he'd just won the lottery and come to share the news. Something was going on and it wasn't good.

"I'm drinking coffee," he answered. "Pour yourself a cup and sit down."

While she took his advice she stole a glance from one brother to the other.

There was a resemblance between Quinn and Logan in their solid boxer builds and coloring—both of them with Lindsey's same dark brown hair and gray eyes. But where Quinn had a face that was a combination of rugged and studious, Logan's was male-model perfect.

"What's up?" Lindsey prompted when she joined them.

Logan answered with an edge of grim sarcasm. "I was given the rest of the day off to consider whether or not to accept my transfer."

"Your request came through and Wortman okayed it?" Lindsey guessed.

It was Quinn who answered her. "The transfer he's been offered isn't the transfer he requested. They want to move him into the rat squad."

"Internal affairs? Cops going after cops?" she asked with a full measure of distaste, knowing it was what Logan had been worried might happen.

"It's either the rat squad or a whole career of parade, dignitary and debutante duty. Those are my options."

"I'm sorry," Lindsey said, meaning it.

"Yeah, me, too," Logan muttered.

"What are you going to do?"

The younger of her two brothers stared into his coffee cup. "I don't know. It may be time to quit the force."

This had been their topic of conversation a lot lately, so she was aware that it wasn't what he wanted to do, and she knew how hard it was for him to even suggest it. "I know we've gone over this before, but you really can join the agency," she reminded in an effort to help. "It is *Strummel* Investigations, you know. You'd fit right in. And you're more than welcome. There's always enough work."

Quinn said, "That's what I've been telling him."

Logan nodded slowly. "I'm seriously thinking about it this time."

And the decision was his to make so there was nothing more either Lindsey or Quinn could say.

Silence fell for a long moment. But when Logan broke it, it was to change the subject completely.

"I did get a chance to do some of what you asked me to before Wortman called me in," he said to Lindsey, as if finding respite in thinking about something else. "Unofficially—the way you wanted," he added.

"And?"

"Those babies haven't been reported missing or kidnapped anywhere in Colorado or the surrounding states. I contacted the national bureau of missing children—nothing there, either. My guess is that your client probably is the father, and the mother just figured it was his turn to play parent. I've seen it before. Dad ducked out on her, she tried to support them on her own for a while and either can't do it or doesn't want to. Maybe found greener pastures somewhere and doesn't want the kids grazing at her heels, so she just dumped them on his doorstep."

Lindsey knew Logan was speaking from experience but it still rubbed her the wrong way to hear him categorize Graham so unfavorably. She opened her mouth to set him straight but Quinn cut her off.

"So you took the job?" he asked.

"Basically," she answered offhandedly, turning back to Logan. "Graham Dunn doesn't fit the picture you're painting. He owns Dunnit Tennis Shoes and lives in a very affluent section of Evergreen. He's surprised enough by this whole thing for me to believe that if these kids are his it's the first he's heard of them. He seems to be a nice, decent, responsible man who's just had the shock of a lifetime and is only concerned for the babies' welfare, whether they prove to be his or not."

Logan's eyebrows rose. "Geez, I haven't heard you defend a guy so fiercely since you had that crush on

Pointy-chin Chumson in the eighth grade. If I'd have known you were so touchy about this I would have tiptoed around it.''

Okay, so maybe she had overreacted.

And maybe for reasons not too different than when she was fourteen. Pointy-chin Chumson had been going steady with her best friend, and she'd had no business having a crush on him.

Not that she had a crush on Graham Dunn.

But she had had a hard time not thinking about him since she'd left him yesterday.

Quinn interrupted again. "What does 'basically' mean?" he questioned. "If you 'basically' took this case, did you accept it or not?"

Okay, so she had hedged. Mainly because she'd been having second thoughts. "I accepted it," she said, but there was more of that hedging in her voice that she couldn't seem to eliminate.

"But?" Quinn probed.

"It's no big deal. I'm just not wild about looking into something involving kids right now." Or something involving a client she found so attractive.

"Maybe I should take over," Quinn offered.

She'd seriously considered that at one point, during a long, sleepless night of wholly inappropriate, unprofessional and unwanted thoughts. But just as she had before meeting Graham, she'd rejected the idea.

Three months ago she'd had to bow out of work. After the five that had come before—through which she'd been a basket case, making dumb mistakes, overlooking things that shouldn't have been overlooked and generally doing a lousy job—she'd felt she had to.

But she'd spent that three-month hiatus putting herself and her life back together, and when she signed on

to work again the day before, it was because she believed she was on her feet again. Ready, willing and able—eager, in fact. And if fate intended to test her by throwing her smack-dab in the middle of this case, well, she was up for it. She could do it.

"No, I don't want you to take over, Quinn. It'll be okay. *I'm* okay. I just got accustomed to being a lady of leisure. It's not easy to be a working stiff again," she joked.

Neither of her brothers smiled. They both just went on watching her as if she might crack up at any moment.

She jutted out her bottom lip and bounced her index finger against it, making a lunatic noise to oblige them. Then she laughed. "Buck up, boys, there's nothing to look so worried about. I'm all better."

She stood then, taking her coffee cup with her. "Better get to work. I came to open a file on this case and start a background check on the client just to be sure of what I'm dealing with," she said, glad to hear herself sounding confident, in charge of her own investigation and her own emotions.

Then she added, "I've arranged for a doctor's appointment so the babies can be examined and we can have a blood test done to help determine paternity. Logan, I'd appreciate it if you'd keep an eye out for incoming missing-persons reports—still unofficially, of course."

"Sure," the younger of her two brothers answered.

"Nose to the grindstone," she said, heading for the hall that led to the large room she and Quinn used as the office of Strummel Investigations.

It was his voice that followed her. "Take it easy, Lindsey. You don't have to be Superwoman."

She gave him a mock frown. "No problem," she answered as she left the kitchen.

But maybe that assurance wasn't quite right, after all.

Because in Evergreen there were two babies she was just itching to get her arms around and a man whose every nuance, every tone of voice, every line in his handsome face made her heart beat faster.

Still, though, she couldn't turn this case over to Quinn. She didn't want to.

She just had to do what she could to keep herself emotionally removed from those babies.

And as for being attracted to Graham Dunn?

She'd just think about how miserable she'd been in the past eight months. How much it hurt when relationships failed. How much was lost.

And that would fix that.

LINDSEY HAD ARRANGED for an appointment with a pediatrician for two that afternoon. She'd called Graham to let him know and left a message on his answering machine when he hadn't picked up, thinking he was probably home but too busy to get to the phone.

But at twelve-thirty when she rang his doorbell for the third time without a response, she began to wonder.

No sounds came from inside, and a peek through the picture window showed baby clothes and diapers strewn around the living room, but no other sign of Graham or the babies.

Wondering where he could possibly be, she rang the bell again and then knocked, too. And finally heard movement from within.

Her client opened the door a moment later, dressed in blue jeans that hugged his hips and a bright red polo shirt that left no question about the wide, straight ex-

panse of glorious shoulders. The clothes looked fresh, as if he'd just put them on, but his blue eyes were at half-mast, as if he'd been sleeping. And there was a hint of stubble shadowing his face.

When he recognized her he slid an arm up the door's edge to lean against it in a stance that might have been seductive if he hadn't looked exhausted enough to need the support. Still, there was a sexy quality to his smile as he lazily finger-combed his hair with the other hand.

"If this was the old West you'd be at risk of being shot at this moment," he said in a deep, raspy voice that came from disuse but could have been due to passion under different circumstances. That, together with her wandering thoughts about the way he looked, made her stomach flutter.

She ignored it.

"Late riser?" she guessed.

"As in this being the first time I've been out of my bed since getting in it last night? Oh, nooo." His great lips formed a perfect circle as he nearly sang that, shaking his head in slow motion. He went through an hour-by-hour recounting of how he'd actually spent the time he should have been sleeping, this most recent round having lasted barely forty-five minutes.

After learning what a rough night he'd spent, Lindsey felt guilty for awakening him. And yet, there was another part of her—deep down and untoward—that was appreciating the sight so much she was a little glad, too.

Even though she hated herself for it.

"I came early to make sure we went to the doctor's office prepared," she said.

"We have to prepare for that? I thought we'd just go," he said, his eyes finally opening fully from the hooded stare they'd been giving her.

"The twins will need diapers and a change of clothes in case they wet through what they're wearing on the way, and washcloths—though baby wipes would be better but there weren't any in the bag—for cleanups if they mess, and snacks to keep them busy and quiet, and the security blanket and that monkey I found in the bag yesterday if one of them uses that for comfort—"

"Charlie does," he interrupted. "And I get the idea. Although it's hard to believe it takes so much just to get them out of the house."

He seemed to realize belatedly that he was keeping her standing on the porch and swung out of the way as if he were attached to the door. Or maybe hanging on to it was keeping him on his feet when nothing else would. "Come on in. They're asleep. They seem to do that better in the day than at night."

"You can't let them. A couple of naps are good, but not too many or too long. Letting them sleep until nine last night was your mistake."

"Mmm," he agreed, seeming to drift off standing there.

"Graham?" Lindsey said to remind him he couldn't.

Some rapid blinking brought him out of it and he let go of the door to close it. Then he pressed his back to it as if he'd captured her, and once more Lindsey pushed away on the titillating idea and straightened her thinking.

"We'll need to leave in about half an hour. Did they have lunch before you put them to bed?" she asked.

"Breakfast. Lunch. Brunch. Call it whatever you want. So far today they've tried oatmeal, eggs, granola

bars, cookies, peanut butter, chicken-noodle soup, Vienna sausages, pickles, olives and some kibble Charlie found in the cupboard that I keep to feed the wildlife around here. They liked the kibble the best. What do they actually eat, anyway?''

"After the appointment we'll go to the grocery store and get some things."

"Ah, you're a saint. I was going to beg you on bended knee to do some shopping with me so I'm more outfitted for this, in the way of food and everything else. Cats and dogs fit into people's lives easier than babies do. You'd think being the same species we'd be naturally prepared, but this is like aliens from outer space descending on an ill-equipped earth."

"That bad, huh?" Lindsey said, losing a battle to suppress a smile at his continuing befuddlement.

"Worse."

"Did you get the neighborhood baby-sitter to help you?"

"She's away at boarding school. Left last week. I had to wing it."

Poor babies. Lindsey suffered a wave of guilt for having left them to him. "But you all three survived."

"You could say that. And in the process we even got to know each other a little. Charlie says Kay for Kate, muk for milk and a couple of other things I haven't quite translated yet. Kate calls her brother Chlee, milk is mik and they both say no—loud and clear."

"Did they call for their mother or say anything else that sounds like a name? Anything we might be able to use to figure out who they are?"

"Nothing. Kind of strange, though, now that you mention it, that they didn't ask for their mother."

Lindsey had already considered it. Along with the fact that they weren't afraid of strangers and easily accepted affection from them.

It was possible they'd felt so secure in their short lives that new faces just seemed like an interesting novelty without scaring them.

It was also possible they'd been shuttled around so much they were used to accepting comfort and care from anyone willing to give it.

She liked the first possibility best but couldn't ignore the second and what it might have to do with this case.

"Why don't we pack things up before waking them," she suggested. "If they're tired and cranky a doctor's visit isn't going to be nice."

"Okay. Just let me run a razor over my face. I shaved before dawn today. Five-o'clock shadow is striking early." He worried his beard with a big, capable hand, and Lindsey's gaze trailed along, lingering on his well-defined jawline when it shouldn't have.

"Make yourself at home," he added with a nod in the direction of the living room before he shrugged away from the door.

As he passed by her he bent down close enough to her ear for her to feel the warm brush of his breath and said, "It's good to see you again." Then he turned down the hall to the bedroom.

And Lindsey had to wait for a wave of unexpected pleasure to wash through her before she could actually move from the spot it rooted her to.

He wasn't flirting with her, she told herself firmly. What he'd said could have been said by anyone, to anyone. It was merely a friendly comment.

Delivered as if it had been an intimate one.

No, she was just imagining things.

And she had to get her mind off this path.

This time distraction came easily, for at that moment came a resounding "out!" from down that same hallway Graham had just entered.

And that was all it took to lure her to the guest room where she'd last seen Charlie and Kate.

Careful to be quiet, she slowly pushed open the door and was surprised by what she found. Both babies were awake and standing at the spindled bars of a crib in the middle of the room.

"Hi," Charlie said as if he were thrilled to see her.

"Hi," Lindsey answered with a laugh, crossing to the crib.

"Out," Kate demanded, holding her arms over the rail to Lindsey.

Alarms sounded in her head, reminding her to resist the temptation of these two, but as if she hadn't heard them she picked Kate up and then lovingly smoothed Charlie's feathery hair. "Want to go bye-bye today?" she asked.

"Bye-bye," Kate repeated, giving a giddyap bounce.

"How about we change some diapers first?"

"No. Bye-bye," Kate insisted.

"I should have kept my mouth shut," Lindsey murmured.

There were clean diapers on the unmade bed behind the crib. She got two of them and then lifted Kate back in beside Charlie. "Lie down for me," she said, unsure if they were old enough to understand.

Apparently they were because Charlie complied, and Kate said, "No."

Lindsey lowered the side of the crib and did a quick change of Charlie, ignoring Kate's chant of bye-bye while she did.

When she finished she said, "Charlie's ready to go. If you want to, you'll have to lie down so I can change your pants, too."

This time the little girl did, though she didn't stop the chant.

Lindsey was just resnapping Kate's overalls when Graham found her. He came to stand beside her, hoisting Charlie to his hip as if it were second nature now.

With his hair combed and his face freshly shaven and smelling of cologne, it wasn't easy for Lindsey to resist the powerful effect he had on her. She did it by asking questions.

"How did Charlie get the lump on his head and where did the crib come from?"

Graham explained Charlie's accident with the chairs that had surrounded the bed. It was obvious he felt responsible.

"You couldn't have done anything differently. Besides, kids get a lot of bumps and bruises through the course of things, even when you're doing all you can to keep them safe."

"Thanks," he said. "I needed to hear that."

His gratitude came with a flash of that charming smile of his, and her heart gave a little skip before she tamed it. "And the crib?" she prompted.

"I figured I'd better get one in a hurry so I was on the phone to a store in town when they opened this morning. For a pretty substantial incentive bonus I got this delivered, assembled and the sheets and blankets to go with it. That's how the kids got to sleep this time—I put them in to try it out and they just curled up as if that's what I'd intended for them to do."

"It was probably the time they're used to having a nap," Lindsey guessed, impressed with his initiative and

the extent to which he was willing to go to make these kids at home and safe. She also noted the fact that there was a proprietary air about him today, as if one night alone with Kate and Charlie had begun to form a bond between them. And it occurred to her that whether or not he was their father, given some practice he'd be a good one.

He went on. "I thought it would be okay not to have two cribs—for now, at least. They sleep nearly on top of each other, anyway. That isn't dangerous or anything, is it?"

"It's fine," she assured.

Then, both because she knew it was getting late and to escape this one-woman Graham Dunn admiration society she seemed to have suddenly formed, she checked her watch and said, "We'd better get things packed and go."

And so what if he was slightly slow in taking his eyes off her, as if he were committing every feature of her face to memory and appreciating the process?

Just one more thing her wayward mind was conjuring up.

Wasn't it?

Maybe. But it was Lindsey who had to finally turn away, for he seemed to have no inclination to do it himself.

She scooped up Kate and headed for the door. "No time to waste," she said, hating that she sounded like Mary Poppins, but glad to be on the move and back into more open space, where she hoped she could find some relief from the potent effects of Graham Dunn.

FIFTEEN MINUTES LATER, with a grocery sack full of baby things, Kate in Lindsey's arms and Charlie in Graham's, they were ready to leave.

"I only have a sports car," Graham said as he locked up behind them. "So I guess that means you get stuck juggling both of these bugs on your lap."

"I'm a step ahead of you," Lindsey countered, pointing to her station wagon where two children's car seats were visible in the back seat.

"Looks like you had an expensive morning, too. Make sure you put the cost of those things on my bill."

"I didn't have to buy them. They were in my garage," she said much more softly than she'd intended to.

"For some reason it didn't occur to me that you might have kids," Graham said as they went out to the driveway where she was parked.

"I don't," she said bluntly, opening the rear door to put Kate in one of the seats in question.

Graham went around to the other side and did likewise with Charlie, watching closely what Lindsey did to strap Kate in and performing the same tucks and pulls and snaps until he had Charlie secured, too.

When that was done, both adults got into the front, with Graham settling in to stare at Lindsey as she started the car.

"Does it say somewhere in the private invesigator's handbook that you have to be equipped with things like kids' car seats?" he asked.

"I just happened to have them." She didn't take her eyes off the road, as if this conversation were small talk instead of something that was twisting her stomach into knots.

"You don't have kids but you do have their equipment?"

Lindsey had no intention of getting into this. "Uh-huh," she acknowledged. Then, before he could ask more, she changed the subject. "This morning I spoke to the pediatrician we're going to see. Just so you know, I didn't lead him to think there was anything suspicious about the twins being left with you."

"I hadn't thought about it, but I don't suppose that would be a good idea, no."

"It wouldn't have been a good idea, at all. If he knew they'd been randomly abandoned and we didn't have any idea by whom or why or if they really are yours, he would have to report it."

"Sure, that makes sense."

"I told him that until yesterday you didn't know about them, that their mother sprung this on you and we just want to make sure they're healthy. I also said you want to have a blood test to confirm your paternity if possible, for your own peace of mind and to give you some legal standing with the mother."

"And he accepted that without a problem?"

"He seemed to. He knows me and I assume he trusts what I tell him."

"Then he's a personal friend of yours?"

"No. I've used him professionally."

"Your profession or his?"

He was fishing again and she knew it. But still she wasn't going to let him catch anything. Instead she went on instructing him on how they needed to handle the situation. "This story should cover the fact that you won't know anything about them or their background, even their birth date. We'll say the mother didn't fill you in on any of the details. That your relationship ended

badly before she knew she was pregnant, and you had no idea what was going on until yesterday when she showed up and handed them over to you.''

"And if he gets curious and wants the mother's name and address?'' Graham asked, putting particular emphasis on the word *curious,* clearly letting her know it was just what he was feeling himself.

"That's up to you. You can give the name of the woman you suspect might be their mother or make something up. And either way you can claim you don't have an address for her, that that's why you hired me."

She glanced at him out of the corner of her eye and discovered him smiling at her again.

"I hope you aren't this good at lying in other instances," he said as if there were a personal relationship between the two of them, even if there wasn't one between her and the doctor.

"Not much of it is a lie, really. Just a rough sketch, with the exception of your having had contact with the mother. Or at least that's what you led me to believe yesterday. Am I wrong?'' She gave him a sidelong look that was intended to remind him that he was keeping secrets of his own.

He only smiled at her, leaving her curiosity unsatisfied, too.

Not wanting him to know he was getting to her, she concluded her instructions. "Just be careful not to raise suspicions or the doctor will be obligated to call in the authorities and that nice new crib of yours won't get much use.''

THE TWINS SEEMED to view the doctor's office as high adventure. They attacked the toys in the waiting room like gluttons at a banquet, and were more interested in

playing with the instruments the nurse used to take their temperature, test their hearing and look down their throats, than in letting her do her job.

When the nurse left Lindsey, Graham and the twins to wait for the doctor, Kate and Charlie explored the vinyl-covered examining table that was built into the wall, reveled in tossing the children's books off the edge and seemed to have no qualms at all about being dressed in only their diapers.

Even their first sight of Dr. Taylor barely made them pause, and he was over six feet tall, heavyset and wore braces on his teeth despite the fact that he was well past forty.

Lindsey introduced Graham and the kids, and once the two men shook hands and exchanged amenities, the pediatrician turned his focus on Lindsey once again.

"I was sorry to hear about your divorce. We saw Bobby here in the office yesterday and he talked about it. Quite a coincidence to have him in one day and you the next."

Lindsey felt the color drain from her face. It was bad enough that being here brought back memories of past visits in a capacity completely different than as a detective, but now to hear about Bobby, too.

She stood up a little straighter. "Is he sick? It isn't his tonsils again, is it?" she asked, trying to keep the urgency to know out of her voice.

"He's fine. He just had a cold. And a nasty cough. We gave him some medicine and sent him home."

But even the doctor's reassurance couldn't stop the vise that clenched her heart. Bobby was sick, and she wasn't there to take care of him.

Then, clearly unaware that he'd just dropped a bombshell on her, Dr. Taylor faced the examining ta-

ble and said, "So what do we have here? How about if we take a look at one of you at a time? Lindsey, why don't you show Charlie that pretty picture over there while Dad and I do the first checkup on Kate?"

Lindsey didn't have to be asked twice because more than anything she needed a moment to herself. She grabbed Charlie and took him to the corner of the room.

But it wasn't the animal-shaped alphabet she had any interest in. She was lost in a sudden flood of feelings that had her holding on tight to Charlie, laying her head against the top of his, closing her eyes and trying to fill the void the doctor's words had left in the pit of her stomach, fighting the horrible wish that she could run out of that room and to that other little boy.

Then she suddenly became aware that Graham was watching her from behind the doctor's back. Staring at her, she thought, though since she only caught sight of him peripherally she couldn't be sure.

No doubt he was wondering about what the doctor had said, jumping to his own conclusions. Maybe he was also wondering just exactly what he'd gotten himself for a P.I.—some overly emotional woman driving around with two car seats and no kids to put in them, standing there clinging like mad to this baby who was probably his.

She finally forced herself to meet his gaze, but when their eyes met none of what she'd expected looked back at her from those bright blue ones of his.

She found confusion and more of that curiosity that they'd both danced around earlier. But also warmth and compassion. Kindness. A sort of understanding and acceptance, as if he were saying he knew something had just shaken her up and that she was doing the best she

could to deal with it. That if he could, he'd reach out to take her in his arms, press her head against his chest and just let her absorb his strength until she could regain her own.

Or maybe she was just imagining that part of it.

She curbed the thought, imaginary or not.

This man was her client, she reminded herself even as she went on being lost in his gaze. Not someone to comfort her. And she shouldn't be showing the need to be comforted.

Then the doctor pronounced Kate healthy and right on target developmentally for a fifteen-month-old, breaking the silent connection Graham seemed to have forged with Lindsey.

And while she was grateful the moment had passed, a secret part of her was also sorry when she lost Graham's attention so he could take Kate from the examining table the way the physician asked him to.

"Lindsey?" the pediatrician prompted, apparently having spoken to her before. But she'd been so lost in watching Graham that she hadn't heard him.

"I'm sorry?" she said to let him know she wasn't sure what he wanted.

"It's Charlie's turn," Dr. Taylor told her.

She returned the little boy to the table, took Kate from Graham and went back to the corner.

But when she stole another glance at him she found him looking at her again. Only this time he winked outlandishly, and the smile he tossed her was full of mischief and conspiracy, captivating her so completely she couldn't keep from smiling back.

That was when she realized she actually felt better. That the emotional storm had passed.

And as difficult as it was to believe, and as much as she didn't want to admit it was so, she knew Graham Dunn had had something to do with it, even though they'd never exchanged a word.

IT WAS AFTER SEVEN that evening when Lindsey, Graham and the twins got back to Graham's house. But it took until eight to unload Lindsey's car.

They'd spent the remainder of the day on a shopping spree to end all shopping sprees. It had resulted in Kate and Charlie being outfitted with clothes enough to weather numerous disasters; weighted cups with lids to avoid some of those disasters; tiny spoons—the better to feed them with; crib sheets, blankets and quilts for any fluctuation in temperature; two high chairs; groceries to satisfy the appetites of a whole school full of finicky eaters; and toys, toys and more toys.

Lindsey had cautioned Graham that the babies' mother could come for them at any moment, or that Lindsey could solve the case within a matter of days, cutting their time with him short.

But none of her warnings had had any more effect than her advice to buy things in moderation. Clearly money was not a problem for him, and besides the fact that he seemed to think if he bought every baby gadget he came across he would somehow have all the secrets to dealing with the twins, he seemed to just plain be enjoying himself.

Lindsey couldn't find fault with that, for through it all she'd had some trouble herself remembering this was work. Not only because she didn't usually shop and have dinner out with her client, but because she'd had too much fun for it to feel like a job.

In fact, the day and evening were the best she'd had in a long while. Helped in no small part by the fact that Graham hadn't so much as asked about the things the doctor had said or her reaction to them.

"This was all above and beyond the call of duty tonight," he said as he walked her out to her car once it had been emptied and Kate and Charlie were exploring their new things in the middle of the living-room floor, where he could keep an eye on them through the picture window.

Not that he was doing much of that. His attention was centered on Lindsey with the exception of fleeting glances over his shoulder.

She actually watched the twins from the distance more than he did, though not because it was necessary. It helped keep her own eyes off her client. Something she needed help with, for every hour they'd spent together had left her discovering more and more about him that she found appealing—his sense of humor, his even temper and good nature, his patience with the babies, his generosity, the sexy way he raised one eyebrow and one corner of his mouth at the same time. . . .

And a gazillion other things that were chipping away at her every attempt to remember that her involvement with him was strictly business.

"I enjoyed myself," she answered him in understatement.

"I'm glad. But I still hope you're charging me for gas and mileage and double your usual fee for overtime."

"Oh, at least," she joked, without any intention of actually doing as he suggested. She'd gone off the clock a long while ago—when he'd made her laugh in a way she hadn't for longer than she could recall.

She opened the door to the driver's side and stepped into the shelter of the car without actually getting in. Then she nodded in the direction of the house. "They only napped for that hour in the car this afternoon so they should be about ready to go down for the night, and they'll probably sleep through until morning."

He rested both arms along the rim of the door and leaned slightly forward, toward her. "Those are the sweetest words any woman has ever said to me," he teased as if he'd been hoping to hear something else. "Do I look as if I need the rest?"

He looked terrific. Too terrific for her own good. "Maybe a little ragged around the edges," she lied. Then she tried to get back to business, something there hadn't been much of since leaving the doctor's office. But now she hoped it would yank her out of feeling as if this were the end of a very pleasant date. "I have some things to do at the office tomorrow but I'd like to come in the afternoon to talk to your housekeeper. You did say she'd be here, didn't you?"

"And I thought you might just come over to see me." His grin teased and flirted and let her know he was serious all at once. And flutters of delight went off inside her.

She glanced at the twins to combat it and pretended he hadn't said anything. "I know your housekeeper wasn't here the day the babies appeared, but she might have some ideas about where they came from, or know something we could use."

"If she can help she will. She's a nice lady."

"Good," Lindsey answered distractedly, wondering why, when Graham himself only talked business, she missed the flirting.

Time to get out of there, she told herself, before work and pleasure got any more mixed up. "I better go."

He nodded but it seemed slow and reluctant, and he didn't move so she could actually leave. "Ordinarily," he said, "I wouldn't think of letting a woman leave my house after dark to drive home alone. But I'm stuck." He pointed a thumb over his shoulder to illustrate.

"Ordinarily my clients don't drive me home. At night or any other time," she countered to remind them both of their relationship.

But he only seemed to take it as a challenge, if the glint in his eyes meant anything. "Well, if I could, I'd change that. On this case, anyway."

"I really better go," she repeated in a rush against the little thrill of excitement he was raising in her and what was flashing through her mind, which had never flashed through before about a client—the craving for a goodnight kiss.

She ducked into the car to escape those flashes and the temptation that came with them. "Shall I call before I come tomorrow?"

"You don't need to. I've handed over the reins of Dunnit Tennis Shoes, for the time being, to deal with what's going on here. So here is where I'll be. Just come whenever you're ready."

"That's what I'll do then," she said, too brightly, too breathlessly.

He closed the door but kept his hands hooked on the edge of the window that was half-open, bending over to peer inside. And again images of end-of-date kisses shot through her thoughts.

"Call me if anything happens in the meantime," she instructed.

"How about if I just want to talk to you?"

"About the babies?"

"About anything."

The flutters of delight struck again but she tried to ignore them. "Well, sure," she answered uncertainly.

He must have realized he was unnerving her because he grinned as if it pleased him. "And you can call me, too. Anytime. For any reason. Or for no reason at all."

"If I hear anything I will," she answered, being purposely obtuse.

It only made his grin widen.

But as if he'd teased her enough for one night, he straightened away from the car and hit the roof as a send-off. "Drive safe, Lindsey. I'll be looking forward to tomorrow."

Me, too, she thought. But she started her engine and only said, "Good night," as she backed out of the drive.

"'Night," he called.

She couldn't resist one last look at him as he stood there watching her go. Handsome. Confident. Apparently enjoying himself.

Maybe enjoying her?

Or how unsettled he could make her?

And no matter how firmly she told herself to keep in mind that he was the client, and that even if he weren't he'd be a man with too many complications that struck too close to home, she still couldn't help wondering what it might have been like to be kissed by him. To be taken into his arms, to feel them wrapped around her, holding her close. To have that incredible mouth possessing hers....

Wayward thoughts.

It had been a day full of them.

But in the solitude of her car as she drove home, she just couldn't escape them.

And in the solitude of her bed once she got there, she had an even harder time.

Try as she might.

All night long.

Chapter Three

Not all clients of Strummel Investigations were subject to background checks, but Graham Dunn wasn't the first, either. Lindsey and Quinn would look into a client if an investigation began to uncover things that made it appear the person was lying, and that the lies could incriminate the agency in some wrongdoing. Or if there was just something suspicious about the client.

Graham's reaction to the babies, and their not having been reported missing either locally or nationally, made it seem as if he was exactly what he seemed to be—a man surprised by someone leaving two kids for him to father.

But the fact that there were children involved, and Lindsey was walking a line between what was legal and what wasn't, contributed to her decision to do a background check on her own client.

So that was what she'd spent the day doing.

And as she drove up to Evergreen at four-thirty that afternoon, she considered what she'd found.

Her client was quite a man.

He'd graduated with honors from Stanford, built Dunnit Tennis Shoes from the ground up and used the power, prestige and a fair share of the profits that came

with owning one of the country's most successful businesses to support a number of worthy causes. Not all of them pertained to kids, but a lot did, particularly benefiting the underprivileged and needy.

He contributed to the Make A Wish Foundation, made donations of shoes to recreation centers in depressed areas and personally backed scholarship programs.

Some of the biggest names in sports endorsed his shoes, but only if they kept their noses clean and were honest role models. And he was the owner of numerous season tickets for basketball, football and even Denver's new baseball team, which he donated to youth groups around the city.

He'd funded a hospital wing and purchased an expensive piece of X-ray equipment, and just generally seemed to be a soft touch for whatever need there was that he could help meet in some way.

If a person were going to leave kids on somebody's doorstep, his was a good choice for more reasons than the fact that his home was in a nice area.

Not all of what he did was altruistic, though.

According to his credit report he skied in Aspen, spent a small fortune on airline tickets, hotels and restaurants around the world and generally kept himself well entertained.

And not without female company, was Lindsey's guess when figures reached higher than they would have been for one person alone.

But of specific interest to her was the female company he'd kept two years earlier—a woman whose picture she'd come across in an article about him in a national magazine published four months ago.

There had been several photographs accompanying the script—Graham as a boy with his father, his high school-yearbook picture, standing outside the first manufacturing plant of Dunnit Tennis Shoes, working alongside his employees in the factory, in his current plush office and at home.

And there had also been the one she had with her at that moment.

The caption explained that it had been taken at a banquet for Denver's mayor. Unfortunately it left Graham's companion unnamed.

But the woman could well be the twins' mother. The same woman Graham was protecting from Lindsey's investigation.

Tall, thin and beautiful, in the photograph she was dripping in diamonds. She had long, silky blond hair that could have done justice to shampoo commercials, and a flawless face to go with it.

But more than the woman's looks, what jabbed at Lindsey was the evidence of Graham's affection for her. Both of his arms were wrapped possessively around her waist as if she might have been trying to get out of the shot and he'd insisted she be included.

Oh yes, Lindsey had studied it long and hard. It was burned into her brain. And she had it on the seat beside her as she got on the highway. She intended to hold it up to the twins to check for a resemblance. But she was also going to confront Graham with it to see his reaction.

Even as she drove she couldn't help glancing over at it periodically and hating herself for the feelings it raised in her.

Jealousy.

She could hardly believe it, but that's what the photograph evoked.

First she'd found herself attracted to a client. And now jealous of a woman in a two-year-old picture.

"Way to go," she told herself facetiously.

But she was determined that the odd presence of these emotions would not influence her. She was a professional and she wouldn't let that happen any more than she let her work be affected by disliking a client, as occurred on occasion.

This was going to be tougher than those times and she knew it, but she decided that disliking a client or being drawn to one called for the same response—doing her job efficiently but as quickly as possible.

Which was why she had called to ask the housekeeper to wait for her and was headed into the mountains rather than quitting for the day. Hurrying a case along meant concentrating on that case alone, spending evenings and weekends on it, doing all she could to bring it to a close.

It also meant pursuing a subject her client had expressly avoided—the woman in the picture.

And if she found out that that woman was the love of his life? Someone who had left a gap other women only became a substitute for?

All the better.

Because then she'd know for sure to run the other way.

After all, she'd had experience.

GRAHAM USUALLY liked to jog at dawn but since coming home to find the twins in his bedroom he hadn't been able to do it at all. Even with his housekeeper in today he hadn't found the opportunity until Lindsey

had called and asked that Annie wait for her. By then there had been some organization to his home again, and since the older woman had to stay anyway she agreed to watch the kids while he did a few miles.

It felt great. The air was autumn-kissed, the leaves were turning, and just to have a little time to himself after this bout of impromptu fatherhood was a blessing.

Not that he wasn't enjoying the experience of the twins. Sure, he hadn't chosen it, and God only knew what Lindsey might turn up as the reason the kids had been left with him, or who had left them, but still he was getting a kick out of them.

And that surprised him no end.

He'd spent his adult life working hard. Too hard to pay a lot of attention to relationships, let alone to even think about what it might be like to have children.

Only in the past few years had Dunnit Tennis Shoes reached a point where he felt he could take some time off for anything resembling a personal life—jogging, vacations, relationships.

Well, not really a lot of relationships. A lot of dating, but only one real relationship. The one that may have resulted in Kate and Charlie.

But even when he'd been involved with Lori, he hadn't considered having a family. Just having Lori.

It was ironic, he thought, that the babies might have come out of what had been the best and the worst time of his life.

A time he didn't really want to think about until and unless he had to. So to get his mind off it he took in the scenery, spotting a doe just up the hill beside the road. The animal watched him through wide black eyes as if

he were a curiosity, and he kept her in his view for as long as he could.

Natural beauty.

It made him think of Lindsey.

And though he told himself he should put her out of his mind, too, he found that more difficult than avoiding thoughts of Lori.

Because something between Lindsey and himself had clicked.

He'd felt an instant rapport, a chemistry between them. And each time she stepped into the chaos that was his life right now, the downside of it all disappeared behind his pleasure at her company in it.

Crazy. That really was crazy. There couldn't be a worse time to get into anything personal than when his life had been turned upside down, maybe permanently.

But crazy or not, Lindsey was like a bright light in a dark space, and a single glimpse of her was enough to heat things up inside him in a way that hadn't happened in a long, long time.

Two years, in fact.

That awareness was sobering. And it warned him to keep some control over the attraction to her that could all too easily get away from him. Especially when he factored in that curious business at the doctor's office the day before—her divorce and someone named Bobby. A child, obviously. And also obviously connected to her in some way.

Was he her son?

That might explain her having the car seats they'd used the day before. Or at least one of them. Why had she had two? Was there another child besides Bobby?

And yet she'd said she didn't have any kids at all. Why was that? And why hadn't she known that Bobby

was ill? Even if she didn't have custody, surely she'd still admit to having a child or children and she'd have known one of them was sick.

Or was there more involved than simply not having custody? Was she not allowed any contact at all? Was her claim not to have any kids actually conveying just how completely she'd lost her child? Or children?

But why would any of that be true? Graham asked himself, because none of it struck him as possible in spite of what he had to go on.

From what he'd seen of her with the twins, there was more than her beauty that was natural. Mothering came naturally, too. She was just plain great with kids. Patient, kind, caring, compassionate, protective. No, there hadn't been a single thing about her treatment of Charlie or Kate that hadn't been exemplary.

If this Bobby was her child and she'd lost him, there was another explanation.

But Graham realized he wasn't likely to hear it. At least not anytime soon.

Clearly the subject of her divorce and the boy were open wounds to her, but she'd already made it clear it was none of his business.

Still, the one thing he did know from his own experience was not to get involved with a woman who wasn't free of her past.

So regardless of how well things clicked between them, he knew better than to let this relationship go anywhere beyond her providing investigative services for him.

Gorgeous silver eyes or not. . . .

He'd finished the circuit he normally ran but passed by the road to his house.

Do another mile, he told himself.

Because he knew Lindsey would be there anytime now, and maybe he could run off some of the disappointment and tension he felt at not being able to pursue what had started between them on its own.

Maybe, if he wore himself out physically, he'd actually be able to resist it.

And her.

THERE WAS A yellow sedan in the driveway when Lindsey reached Graham's house. Since she hadn't seen it before, she assumed it belonged to the housekeeper and was glad the woman had waited even though traffic had made the trip longer than anticipated.

Parking alongside the yellow car, Lindsey took the picture of Graham and the beautiful blonde and got out, all the while consciously trying to curb her eagerness to see her client again and reminding herself it was the housekeeper she was here to interview.

And that was who answered the door.

She was a woman in her mid-sixties, medium height, with graying brown hair cut as short as a man's, a slightly plump body and a face that was high-cheekboned and bore traces of youthful loveliness in the handsomeness that remained.

"You must be Lindsey, the detective," she greeted her.

"Yes," Lindsey answered, leaving silence as encouragement for her to identify herself.

"I'm Annie Mafferty, Graham's housekeeper."

"I'm happy to meet you."

The woman stepped out of the way and said, "Won't you come in? Graham told me you had some questions you wanted to ask me. Although I don't know what I can tell you. When I got here this morning and saw

those babies, and Graham explained how he'd found them, you could have knocked me over with a feather. Imagine anyone abandoning those two little darlings.''

"Is Graham here?" Lindsey heard herself ask, sounding much too anxious.

"He went out for a jog just a bit ago. He made sure I knew the babies wouldn't be left to me to take care of since that isn't what he hired me for, but I told him I didn't mind keeping an eye on them while he had a few minutes to himself. From the look of the place when I got here and the sound of what's gone on the last couple of days, I thought he could use a break," she said with a laugh.

Apparently Annie Mafferty was a talker. It made Lindsey's job a lot easier than when people she had to question were shy or withdrawn or reticent. But that wasn't the only reason she liked this lady almost at once. There was a warmth and vitality about her.

Annie closed the front door and went down the center hallway toward the rear of the house. "I have Charlie and Kate on the sun porch.''

Lindsey hadn't been beyond the kitchen before, but Annie took her past it now, into a large family room dominated by a big screen television, some impressive stereo equipment, an overstuffed couch and two chairs that looked as if a person could get lost in them.

From there oak French doors opened to what the housekeeper had referred to as the sun porch one step below—an all-glass solarium full of plants and wicker furniture that gave it a Victorian air.

In the center of the tan-carpeted floor were Kate and Charlie, both too busy trying to tear the clothes off a doll to look up.

It was just as well, Lindsey told herself, because it helped her fight the urge to go to them, to hug them hello, to sit and play with them.

Annie went to a high wing-backed chair, picked up the knitting she'd obviously set there when she'd come to answer the door and sat down. She began her work again as if without even thinking about it.

Lindsey sat at one end of a nearby love seat but didn't jump right in with questions about the babies or Graham. It was better to put people at ease with small talk first. Even people like Annie who didn't seem to need an icebreaker. "What are you making?"

"It's a sweater," the housekeeper answered simply, holding it up to show off the intricate cables she was making out of a hunter green yarn. "Do you knit?"

Lindsey laughed. "No. My mother tried to teach me but I ended up using the needles to have sword fights with my brothers."

"I always have some project or another going. It relaxes me. How many brothers do you have?"

"Two. Both older."

"And sisters? Do you have any of those?"

"I always wanted one but I'm afraid my folks didn't comply." Lindsey paused a moment and then eased into her interview. "So tell me what your job as Graham's housekeeper involves."

"Oh, some of everything," the older woman answered. "I come in three days a week to clean and do the laundry and cook a few things he can reheat for himself. If he needs work done around the place I call for a repairman and oversee that. Sometimes if he's going to entertain I arrange for the caterer. Wife things, I guess you could say is what I do."

"And how is Graham as a boss?" And was that question really relevant to the investigation or was she just trying to have her own opinion of him confirmed?

"I can vouch for his character, if that's what you're wondering about," Annie said without skipping a beat. "Granted I haven't known him long and I'm only an employee, but I think the world of him. He's easy to work for. He isn't messy or demanding, and he lets me know he appreciates me so much, I think he forgets what I'm doing is my job," she said with another of those laughs that Lindsey decided were affectionately wry.

"How long have you worked for him?"

"Only a few months. Since May."

"Do you work for other people, too?"

"No, only here. It supplements my retirement and keeps me just busy enough. When I wasn't working at all, the days just ran into one another. Sometimes I'd wake up in the morning and wonder what the point was in even getting out of bed and putting my clothes on. Now my weeks have structure—three days I have a purpose and that makes me appreciate the four days off. Funny how that is, isn't it?" she asked, then went on without waiting for an answer. "Oh, but I enjoy taking care of people. When you spend your life doing that and suddenly find yourself without anyone to look after, it can be very hard."

"Mmm. Yes it can," Lindsey agreed because she knew exactly what the woman meant. But she had to admire Annie for not wallowing in the leisure that hadn't suited her and doing something about it. "Are you a widow?" she guessed.

"Sad to say."

"Children?"

"A son and a daughter."

"Grandchildren?"

"No, though I wish I could say differently."

"Have you ever seen these babies before?"

Annie laughed slightly. "No, I haven't," she said as if the question hadn't needed to be asked.

"Did Graham show you the note that came with the babies?"

Annie nodded in the direction of the kitchen. "It's in there. It reminded me of those magazine giveaway notices that come in the mail. It might as well have said, Congratulations, Graham Dunn, You Could Be Our Next Lucky Winner, as if a computer filled in the name."

"So you think Graham was just chosen at random?"

"Oh, don't go by anything I think. I don't know. It's just that he's a very informal man. He insists that everyone call him Graham, so it seemed to me that if whoever left the babies was somebody he knew, they'd have only used his first name, not 'Graham Dunn' like it came out of a phone book."

She had a point. "What about someone who doesn't know him well—a repairman, a delivery person, a caterer, anyone who might have seen the way he lives, or known he was a generous, responsible man who could do well by the kids?"

"That could be anybody."

"Okay, but try to think if someone might have mentioned something that could have meant the thought occurred to them. Maybe a comment about all Graham can provide or sharing the good life. Or think if anyone has hit some rough times or changes at home, lost a job or gotten a divorce maybe, or had a spouse

run out on them. Anybody who's worrying how to make ends meet, how to support their family."

Annie stopped knitting and seemed to consider all the possibilities. Then she shook her head. "Nothing. I'm sorry. I guess I do most of the talking and don't really leave much room for other people to."

"What about Graham's friends or relatives? Women you might have met?" Again Lindsey felt uneasy about her own question. But delving into things was what she'd been hired to do. The trouble was, the answers to some of them held more personal interest than they should have.

But again Annie shook her head. "I haven't met many of Graham's friends or relatives or the women he dates. I'm here alone during the weekdays for the most part."

"How about a resemblance?" Lindsey asked. "Do you notice that the twins look like anyone you might have seen here, or a face you've run across in a picture when you've been cleaning?"

Once again Annie stopped knitting, this time to study Charlie and Kate. "I don't see anything about them that strikes me as familiar. I also don't think they look like Graham. Do you?"

Lindsey had been avoiding watching the darling duo in order to maintain her distance and professionalism. But she didn't have a choice then. She glanced over at them as Charlie tried to put a doll stocking on Kate's head while Kate held very still to let him.

Lindsey couldn't help smiling and feeling some of her best intentions to keep her distance from them melt away. "No, I agree. I don't see Graham in them."

"Lucky kids." Graham's deep voice filled the room, surprising everyone in it.

Lindsey's gaze went from the babies to him. He was standing at the French doors. His hair was sweat-damp and dark circles ringed the underarms of a disreputable red T-shirt with the sleeves whacked out of it and the neck sliced in the middle all the way to midtorso. His jogging shorts were only old jeans cut off high on massive, hairy thighs and left ragged around the edges. And slung over a broad shoulder was a towel he must have used to wipe the perspiration from his face, though beads of it still clung to the hair on his chest where his shirt had flapped open to reveal it.

He looked awful.

And, to Lindsey's eyes, too wonderful for anyone to argue that Charlie and Kate wouldn't be fortunate to grow up resembling him.

"What do you think?" Lindsey asked him before she lost herself and her train of thought to this blasted attraction she felt. "Do you think they look like anyone?"

"I've been watching for signs of that myself," he said as he stepped down into the room. "But I don't see anything either."

Lindsey took the photograph of Graham and the woman from where it rested atop her purse, looking from it to the babies and back again.

"What's that?" Graham asked as he came to stand beside her.

"An old picture I found of you."

He bent over for a closer look, frowned and then straightened up again as if he didn't need or want to see more of it. "They don't look like that, either," he said evenly, giving nothing away—if there was, indeed, anything to give away. But he also didn't offer any information on the woman in the photograph.

"Let me see," Annie suggested, reaching over for it. "I know this picture. It was in the article I read at my dentist's office, the one that said Graham's housekeeper had just quit and he was looking for a new one to work only a few days a week. I read that, saw the pictures of how beautiful his home is and how nice it is up here and I got to thinking that a part-time position in a place like this would suit me very well. It's what made me decide to apply for the job." As she talked, the older woman glanced from the picture to the twins. "No, I wouldn't say they look like her, either," she finally said as if settling a debate.

Then she gave Lindsey the photo and stuffed her knitting in a tapestry contraption that was part purse, part stand, snapping the wooden frame closed to carry it by. "If no one needs me for anything else, I think I'll set the table for dinner and be on my way."

Graham hadn't taken his eyes off Lindsey since his glimpse of the picture. While she knew it because she could feel them boring into her, she'd been watching the housekeeper rather than acknowledge his stare.

Now she hazarded just a glance, finding his expression serious, his brows beetled. That photograph had not made him happy. And neither had the fact that she'd dug it up.

His gaze didn't waver even as he spoke to Annie. "Set a place for Lindsey, too," he instructed in what sounded like an ominous tone. "She and I need to talk. It might as well be over dinner."

Lindsey raised a challenging eyebrow at what was more a command than an invitation, but she didn't balk. She was too curious about what he had to say that had been spurred by the picture.

"Won't that be nice," Annie said, either oblivious to her employer's sudden change of mood or trying to lighten that mood. "Then you'll have help feeding the twins, and I won't have to worry that I should have stayed."

Graham didn't answer her. But she didn't seem to notice as she headed for the French doors.

"If you think of anything else to ask me, Ms. Strummel, feel free to call me at home. Graham has my number."

That was excuse enough for Lindsey to escape Graham's scrutiny by standing and taking a business card to the older woman. "My name is Lindsey. And if you should think of anything—even something that seems too minor to be important—I'd appreciate your contacting me about it."

Annie assured her she would, tucking the card into her knitting bag. Then she said her goodbyes and left.

Lindsey had no choice but to turn back to Graham, who had adjusted his own position to go on staring at her.

But he didn't vent his displeasure when he finally spoke. Instead he said in a tight, formal voice, "Would you mind keeping an eye on the twins while I shower?"

Lindsey met him eye-to-eye as if he were the one on the spot. "I suppose I could do that."

He only turned and followed Annie out then, saying nothing else. And Lindsey had the impression that he needed to keep quiet and get away from her to gain some control before he addressed the subject of the picture.

"See?"

She looked down to find Kate had brought her a doll shoe. "I see," she answered, feeling what was now a

familiar clutch of her heart whenever she had contact with these two. "Can you say shoe?"

"No."

That made Lindsey laugh. "Don't you even want to try?"

"No."

Kate took the toy back to Charlie as if it had only been on loan, then sat on the floor again—or actually plopped down. There was no grace to it, it was more that she jutted her well-padded posterior and just dropped.

Left alone with them, Lindsey ignored all her silent warnings to herself and joined them on the carpet.

"Baby," Charlie offered, displaying the now-naked doll.

Kate took it from him, put it and the clothes in Lindsey's lap and said something in gibberish that Lindsey understood as an order for her to dress the doll.

Lindsey complied but as she did she said, "I know this game. I put all this stuff back on, tie the little bows, fasten the snaps, make it pretty, and you guys take it off again."

Which was just what they did, quicker this time than the first.

But Lindsey didn't mind. Not even when they gave it to her to dress as soon as they had. She was enjoying just being on the floor with them. Breathing in the scent of baby powder, listening to them chatter in a language only they understood, watching their tiny hands and the intent expressions on their cherub faces.

How could anyone have willingly given them up? she asked herself for what must have been the hundredth time.

She ached to gather them into her lap, to kiss their downy heads, feel the plump silk of their skin, lay her cheek against their cool, chubby ones.

But she fought it.

They weren't hers. And never again would she let herself get too involved with kids that weren't, even if she did give in to an occasional weakness to be near Kate and Charlie.

Kitchen sounds came then and she realized Graham had had plenty of time to shower and change and he was probably setting out supper.

"Might as well face the music," she told the babies. She stood and held out a hand to each of them. "Come on. Let's go see what Graham's up to."

"Gam," Charlie repeated, his expression brightening as if it were the magic word, while Kate's eyes lit up as if she'd just heard Santa on the roof.

"Do we have some hero worship going already?" Lindsey surmised, glad to know she wasn't the only one affected by the magnetic charm of her client.

She felt as if she were shuffling two penguins as she urged the kids along, for that was how they walked. But when they finally reached the kitchen she found she'd been right about Graham being there.

He was taking a pot of stew out of the oven to set on the stove top. Once he'd done that he went to the refrigerator to unload it of a number of other foodstuffs, but he didn't immediately acknowledge Lindsey's arrival with the twins.

She decided to wait him out, watching him closely as she did.

The shower had done him good. He wore a clean pair of hip-hugging jeans and a crisp navy blue sport shirt. His hair glistened, his face was clean shaven and a hint

of woodsy-smelling cologne mingled with the scents of stew and fresh-baked bread.

The shower also seemed to have helped his temper because when he finally glanced at her his expression was more mildly displeased than angry.

"So you did some investigating of me," he said without preamble.

"It isn't unusual," she lied just a little. "Especially when a client isn't completely open with me. And in this particular situation—when kids are involved and I'm not quite following the letter of the law—I thought it was best if I made sure of a few things."

"Such as?"

"That you aren't a known molester or baby broker, for starters."

"And if, in the process, you just happened across a name I chose not to give you, I suppose that would have been an accident?"

"I didn't."

"I know you didn't. That picture is the only one that was ever taken and there was no name with it."

Ooh, she had struck a nerve. And why was he so sure there were no other pictures and the woman was anonymous? "You know, I won't contact her until you give the go-ahead, but I could be doing some preliminary checking—into her background, what she might have been up to in the last two years."

"If it looks like the kids are mine, then you can get into that."

Was he taking this protective tack because he still had lingering feelings for this woman? Or was she something so special he didn't want her bothered by a P.I.'s nosy questions? Both thoughts left Lindsey fighting a wave of that jealousy that had followed her there.

"I just can't figure out why it's important to keep a secret of the most likely explanation for the twins."

He'd been spooning applesauce into one bowllike section of a baby dish and he stopped to frown directly at her. "Nobody gets to where you and I are in our lives without a couple of things in their past they aren't proud of. Being involved with that woman two years ago is one of mine. The worst of them." Then he added very pointedly, "Surely you, of all people, understand about not wanting to get into something like that when it's over and done with if I don't absolutely have to."

She could have taken issue with that. After all, he was referring to what she'd chosen not to tell him as if it were the same thing and she should respect his privacy the way he had respected hers.

But it wasn't the same thing. He'd hired her to ask questions, to open up his past—good and bad—to find an answer to the babies being left with him. Her past didn't have a role in that. Even if it had raised its ugly head to taunt his curiosity.

But the fact was, the day before he *had* offered her the courtesy of not questioning what had happened at the doctor's office. She owed him that.

"Okay. For now," she said. "But if the blood tests come back—"

"I know. Then I'll tell you who she is."

"Fair enough."

"Good, then we're through with our first fight and we can put it behind us."

The charm was back in a crooked, wry smile. And Lindsey had to suffer the thrill that danced down her spine in response.

It helped to attend to settling Kate and Charlie into their high chairs, tying bibs around their necks while Graham brought the food to the table.

"Let's talk about something else," he suggested as they each took a chair near a baby and began spooning tiny bites of stew into their mouths as if they'd been taking care of the tots together forever.

"Tell me about your housekeeper," Lindsey said. Business—that was always her way out.

Graham complied, though he didn't know much that Annie hadn't already told her.

"She's a nice lady," he added at the end. "Cheerful, willing to do whatever I ask of her, and she's good at her job. I don't have any complaints."

"How did the babies react to her when they initially saw her today?"

He shrugged. "The same as they did to you and me. They didn't rush into her arms as if she were their long-lost mother, if that's what you mean." He leaned slightly forward and said confidentially, "Besides, I could be wrong, but I think she's too old to have babies."

Lindsey smiled but didn't let him distract her. "What about her family? Do you know anything about her son or daughter?"

"I didn't know she had a son or daughter."

"Did she seem to know anything about the twins— their schedule, what they like to eat—that you hadn't told her before? Or did you notice anything in her response to them that seemed overboard or attached or out of the ordinary?"

"On that count you're more suspicious than she is."

He didn't say that with any kind of malice, but with an acceptance that again seemed to keep it just be-

tween the two of them. She appreciated that and conceded his point.

She also thought that from what she'd seen, Graham's observations of his housekeeper were right on target, too. She hadn't fussed over Kate and Charlie any more than any stranger might have, and the twins hadn't seemed bonded to her, either.

"I can't believe Annie would do something like this, anyway. She's a mother hen. Besides, I don't know where she'd have come up with these two. Lord knows, she talks my ear off when I'm here at the same time she is and I've never heard her mention anything that would link her to the twins."

Which put them back to square one and the mystery blonde in the picture.

But Lindsey had granted a temporary moratorium on that subject, so she didn't go back to it.

Instead Charlie began to refuse what she was feeding him and demanded "awkoosh," and both she and Graham turned their deductive powers to figuring out what that could be.

By the time they discovered it was ice cream they'd fallen into small talk about the babies. That lasted through cleaning the kitchen together and getting the twins ready for bed.

Father or not, Graham could have competed with the best of proud, doting papas, Lindsey realized as he continued to regale her with their accomplishments. In fact, his rookie status made him think even things a real parent took for granted were exceptional, including that they had learned his name.

"I felt pretty ridiculous teaching them, though," he confided as he diapered Kate for the night and Lindsey performed the same service for Charlie. "I found my-

self talking to them the way people do in foreign countries, as if speaking very loud and really slowly will cross the language barrier. I was the ugly American in Paris," he joked, mixing titles.

Lindsey could just see it. The image made her smile and she liked that he didn't take himself too seriously to admit it. "It must have worked because Charlie said it for me earlier."

"I taught him something else, too," Graham informed her with a hint of mischief in his blue eyes.

"What?" she asked, feeling like a fish taking the bait.

She had Charlie standing on the bed in front of her by then as she snapped the top of his pajamas.

"Give Lindsey a kiss, big guy," Graham urged.

That was all it took for the toddler to grab her ears like the handles on a loving cup and butt her mouth with his.

Lindsey laughed. "Oh, thank you," she told Charlie with only a slight edge of sarcasm to her voice. Then to Graham she said, "Great technique. Did you teach him that, too?"

He was heating her with a megawatt grin. "It's all his own. Actually I didn't teach him any of it. Last night when I was putting them to bed I asked them if they'd like a kiss, thinking maybe they'd like me to give them one. Instead, Kate gave me a very ladylike peck on the cheek, but Charlie did that."

"And you wanted to take credit for it?"

"No, I just wanted an excuse to get him to do it to you."

"Gee, thanks."

They were finished dressing them for bed and each put a baby into the crib. Lindsey smoothed both tiny brows and said good-night, heading for the door be-

fore the temptation to do more became too strong to resist.

But once she got there she glanced back to find Graham talking very soothingly to them about sweet dreams as he tucked their blankets around them. Then he leaned over the crib side and placed fatherly kisses to the tops of both heads.

But even after that he didn't leave them. For a moment more he stood there, watching them as if marveling at them, before he finally joined her, turning off the light and pulling the door only half-closed.

As Lindsey headed down the hallway she said, "You're getting attached to them."

"You say that so ominously," he answered from behind.

Lindsey shrugged. "There's a good chance you'll have to give them up, you know. That whoever left them will come back for them or that we'll find out they aren't yours and they'll have to be turned over to social services as abandoned kids. You'll be in for a rough ride if that time comes."

"Sounds like something you know all about."

She'd walked right into that one, hadn't she? But she only said, "It isn't something you want to go through." Or something she was willing to ever experience again herself. Which was why she kept trying to resist the "little darlings," as Annie called them.

She gathered up her purse from a table near the entranceway, where she'd set it when Kate had retrieved it from the sun porch during dinner cleanup. Graham's gaze followed her every move, studying her, she knew. But she didn't meet that gaze until she'd opened his front door. Then, her hand still on the knob, she raised her eyes to his oh-so-blue ones, finding she was right.

"I keep wondering if you're okay," he asked with a small, thoughtful smile that only curled one corner of his mouth.

"I'm fine."

He kept on watching her for another moment, as if he could tell by looking whether or not she was lying. Then he must have decided to accept her reassurance because his smile turned full-fledged. "Good. I like you too much for you not to be."

It sounded like a joke making light of the truth. And it pleased her much, much more than it should have.

He lifted a hand to brush her bangs away from her eyes with a single index finger in a gesture that somehow seemed as if he'd been doing it forever.

His eyes captured hers, making a contact that was so strong it was tangible, holding her in the electric warmth of their intense blue color. And Lindsey lost herself in them.

Then he drew that same finger along the very edge of her hairline and around her ear, leaving a trail of tingling sensations before he slipped his hand to cup the back of her head, cradling it, exerting a slight bit of pressure to bring her face nearer to him.

She could have pulled away.

But she didn't. And no amount of telling herself to made any difference.

Then he kissed her.

Maybe it shouldn't have surprised her at that point, but it did.

She recovered herself quickly, though, and before she knew it, she was kissing him back—but hanging on like crazy to that doorknob as if to keep herself apart from him at the same time.

But what a kiss!

Charlie could definitely take lessons in technique, and Graham could own the world with it.

His lips were warm and slightly moist. Parted only enough to make it interesting as he lazily plied her mouth with sweetness.

It was just plain terrific.

So terrific that when he ended it her chin tilted upward all on its own, like a flower following the sun for more of its rays.

She caught herself before it was too apparent, opened her eyes and drew away as if she'd been the one to stop it—the way she should have been.

"I think I've wanted to do that since the first time I let you in here," he said in a deep, quiet voice that was so intimate, so sexy, it licked her nerve endings. Yet even so, he was frowning as though something troubled him.

She heard herself mutter about client-investigator relations, but he only chuckled and she had the sense that he agreed with her in theory but didn't believe it carried any real weight.

"Somehow I think we've been redefining those relations from the start," he said, managing to make that sound deliciously devilish, unwittingly doing even more to weaken her professionalism—if there had been any of it left to weaken.

"I have to go," she said, the first words she'd gotten out that weren't feeble.

He nodded knowingly and took a step backward, not far, only giving her a little breathing room. "Will I see you tomorrow?" he asked in a way that didn't sound as if it had anything to do with the case.

"The results of the blood test should be in," she said as if it were an answer.

"I'll take that as a yes."

She told herself to set him straight about how out of line that kiss had been. To tell him in no uncertain terms not to do it again.

But as she looked up into that ruggedly handsome face with its glinting blue eyes what she really wanted was for him to do it again right that moment.

She cleared her throat. "I'll be in touch," she said, hating the choice of words as soon as they hit the air. To her ears the breathy tone they'd come out on was an indication of just how much touching she was thinking about right then.

"Good night," she added in a hurry, making a quick exit into the evening air, which felt even cooler than it was against the heat of her skin.

She made a beeline for her car and got in it before looking to see if he'd followed her.

He had, but only as far as the end of the porch, where he was leaning a shoulder against a porch post, arms crossed over his chest, smiling at her.

Oh, she really was losing her grip, she thought as she started the engine and backed out of the driveway. First showing signs of weakness over those babies and now this—kissing a client, of all things. And not telling him never to do it again.

She stole just one more glance at him, and when he caught her at it he slipped a big hand out from under the other arm and waved. And there was something even in that that said it was only a matter of time before what happened tonight happened again.

No doubt about it, she absolutely should have told him this couldn't be.

She really should have.

And yet, as she lost sight of him she knew that there was only one problem with that.

If she had, he might have taken her seriously.

Chapter Four

Annie answered the door once again when Lindsey arrived at Graham's house the following day.

"I didn't know if you'd be here or not," Lindsey said as the older woman let her in.

"Normally I wouldn't be, but Graham asked me to come in extra for a while. And it's a good thing I did. You should have seen the mess I walked in on when I got here," she said with a laugh. "Somebody threw a bowl of oatmeal at the wall at breakfast and Kate had just piled spaghetti on Charlie's head at lunch." Annie leaned in confidentially. "Graham hasn't gotten the hang of feeding them both at once and apparently things got out of hand. It's a good thing you were here for dinner last night or Lord knows what else I'd have had to scrape off the kitchen floor."

"Where is he?" Lindsey asked, suppressing a smile.

"He has the twins in his bathroom," Annie said. "Go on back—it's through his bedroom, the only door on the right. He bathed them one at a time yesterday, but today they were so grimy he decided to put them both in the tub at once. Some of the sounds that have been coming from there haven't been good. He may need help and I have my hands full in the kitchen."

That said, the housekeeper headed there, leaving Lindsey no choice but to go to Graham's room.

The door was open when she reached it, but still she tapped on the jamb with the knuckle of one finger, peering inside from the hallway.

The bedroom was huge and all done in brown and navy blue, with a Southwestern accent to the pattern in the quilt that covered an enormous bed.

But there was no answer to her knock, no sign of Graham and only fresh diapers and baby clothes on the bed as evidence of the kids.

From the open door beyond a massive bureau came some of those sounds Annie had mentioned—mainly Graham's voice in abbreviated, unfinished sentences that ran together.

"No, don't— Not soap, Kate, don't eat— Sit down, Charlie— No, not on Kate— It's all right, he didn't mean to— Don't eat the soap! Don't suck the washcloth, either— No! Don't throw it! Oh, good shot—I needed that. Come on, let me wash your face. No! Don't splash. It isn't funny—"

This time Lindsey couldn't suppress a smile even before she stepped to the bathroom doorway to see what was going on in there. One look at it and the smile became a full-fledged grin.

The bathroom was large and all tiled in navy and tan to match the bedroom. It was monopolized by an oval tub that took three steps to get to and would comfortably hold two adults. But at the moment messy baby clothes, wet diapers, and already-damp towels were strewn over the floor. And in the tub were the twins, not taking their bath seriously at all.

Poor Annie, she'd have to go from cleaning the kitchen to cleaning in here, Lindsey thought.

With his back to the door, Graham knelt on the step second from the top to reach the kids, but he didn't have enough hands to do everything at once and the minute he tried washing one of them, the other got into mischief. Wet, sloppy mischief that had splattered water far and wide.

"Come on, guys," Graham cajoled in frustration. "Just sit still and let me— No, Charlie, you can't get out yet— I know you don't want me to wash your ears but there's spaghetti in— Don't spit, Kate, I told you not to eat the soap—"

Kate flung the bar into the water and the splash made a direct hit in Graham's face. He groaned and wiped it on the sleeve of the T-shirt he wore. That was when he caught sight of Lindsey in the doorway—at about the same time her gaze dropped to the derriere that happened to poke out at her when he'd reared away from the tub, a derriere that was the best she'd ever seen grace a pair of faded jeans.

"Lindsey!"

She amended the direction of her glance in a hurry. "I knocked but you must not have heard me," she said to let him know she'd tried to warn him of her presence.

"Bath time," he said with a nod at the twins. "It's dangerous business. If I were you I wouldn't come any closer."

She took his advice and stayed leaning against the doorjamb. Her jeans could withstand a dousing, but she was wearing a white silk shirt and it would turn transparent when wet. Just the way Graham's T-shirt had, she realized as her eyes fell to his chest when he angled in her direction.

Besides, messy or not, the bath looked like altogether too much fun for her to indulge in with those babies when she was trying so hard to keep herself removed.

"Kate is all done," he went on. "Could I dry her off and persuade you to take her in the other room to cut down on some of the havoc in here?"

So much for keeping herself removed. But what could she say? "Sure. And then we need to talk."

He lifted Kate out of the water without a towel at the ready and the little girl began shivering almost at once while she waited for him to retrieve one from a linen closet across the room. Seeing this, Lindsey's heart went out to the baby and that did away with the shored-up resistance she'd come here with today even before she got her hands on the child.

When Graham brought Kate to her—finally wrapped in a towel—Lindsey wasted no time in holding her close.

"I'm almost through with the big guy," Graham assured her as he went back to the tub. "You probably saw the diapers and clean clothes on the bed. I'll be there in a minute, but if you have the urge to get started on Kate I won't mind."

Lindsey laughed at his obvious frazzledness but was more than willing to escape the sight of that well-defined chest cupped by that wet T-shirt. "Sure," she repeated, spinning away before her gaze glued itself there permanently.

Lindsey had only diapered Kate when Graham joined her. She was standing at the foot of his big bed rub-drying the baby's hair. He went around the corner to the side and set a towel-swaddled Charlie on the quilt as if he and Lindsey were sharing a worktable.

Then he straightened, x-ed his arms across his middle and pulled his T-shirt off in one swipe, leaving his upper half bare as he bent to the child again.

There was nothing sexual in the act. It had been purely a matter of necessity—the shirt was drenched. But even unwittingly, there was something very sensual in it. And it didn't help that Lindsey's eyes drank in what was revealed.

Wide, hard biceps that rolled into broad shoulders. Well-honed pectorals speckled with just enough light brown hair to be intriguing. A flat stomach with only a hint of a line of more of that hair trailing from his navel to disappear behind the waistband of his jeans....

It was a glorious sight and Lindsey's mouth went dry as spontaneous memories of his kiss the night before flashed through her mind and the intimacy of being in his bedroom suddenly struck her.

"What do we need to talk about?" he asked.

The sound of that low, rich voice jarred her back to her senses. She forced her gaze away from him and began dressing Kate. "The pediatrician called a little while ago," she answered, and though she couldn't trust herself to look directly at him, peripherally she saw him pause in the middle of diapering Charlie.

"And?" Graham prompted.

"The twins are both AB-negative. The same blood type you have."

Without saying a word he went back to fastening Charlie's diaper. Then, quietly and more to himself than to her, he said, "So they are mine."

Lindsey didn't know whether to extend condolences or congratulations. Instead she offered the truth. "A blood test isn't absolutely conclusive. Granted, that's a

fairly rare type, but you aren't the only person in the world who has it.''

''Coupled with the note, I'd say there isn't much doubt left.''

''It would help if the mother confirmed that you're the father.''

And they both knew what that meant.

Lindsey didn't say more. She merely continued dressing Kate, keeping an eye on Graham through what he was doing.

He put on Charlie's shirt but he was clearly distracted because he twice buttoned it wrong before he got it right.

''Maybe I should just accept that they're my kids and leave it at that,'' he said, as if thinking out loud.

''You mean keep them, raise them and not look into any more about where they came from?''

''Yes.''

''You can't do that,'' she told him bluntly. ''There are things you need to know—birth dates, inoculations, delivery and health histories. To get them into school you'll need their birth certificates. Plus there are legal ramifications. You can't just keep them like stray cats. Either the mother needs to relinquish custody or you have to petition the court for acknowledgment of paternity and custody or guardianship. Besides, you said you wanted this done the right way. The right way is to do all we can to find out what exactly is going on with these kids.''

He maneuvered a pair of tiny overalls around Charlie's diaper without comment. Lindsey knew he was mulling what she'd said and she left him to it.

When she was through with Kate she sat on the bed and finally looked directly at Graham again. His ex-

pression was troubled, but she didn't know if it was in response to the idea of actually being the twins' father or if it had more to do with having to reveal the woman who might be their mother.

Still she kept silent.

And silence was what remained even after Charlie's clothes were on.

Graham took the wet towels into the bathroom. When he returned he pulled a fresh, cream-colored shirt from a hanger in the closet and shrugged into it as if he'd forgotten he had an audience.

Lindsey told herself not to watch. She even looked at the babies instead. But their bath seemed to have tired them out and they were both content to just lie there for the moment, leaving them a poor diversion.

Before she knew it, her willful eyes had drifted back to Graham, who was obviously oblivious to the powerful effect he had on her or the intimacy of the two of them being in the bedroom while he put on his shirt.

Fortunately he managed to do it fairly quickly, buttoning it correctly on the first try and easing a little of her inner turmoil over his naked chest.

Only as he was rolling the long sleeves to his elbows did he speak again. "Her name is Lori Springer," he said, frowning into the distance as if he could see the other woman there. "She lives about half an hour from here. In a Lakewood suburb."

Lindsey fought the rise of that jealousy that had reared its ugly head when she'd found the picture the day before.

"I met her two and a half years ago at a charity dinner," Graham went on. "The relationship lasted seven months. But not until the last few weeks did I know she was married."

"Oh." For some reason Lindsey hadn't expected that.

He was tucking in his shirt with sharp, almost angry jabs into the waistband of his jeans, and she was having trouble assimilating this news while her mind wandered to images of what the rest of him looked like without clothes.

Then, when he'd finished with the shirt, he jammed his fingers through his hair and joined her and the twins on the bed, sitting at the top, his back against the headboard, one foot on the floor and the other propped on that knee.

He was a good distance away, and as lost as he was in thoughts of his past, there wasn't anything any more intimate about them sitting on the bed together than there had been in his removing his shirt before.

And yet, the feel of his weight on the mattress reverberated through her as if there were.

"How did she keep her marriage from you for so long?" she prompted, both to get him going again and to yank her own thoughts back on track.

"Lori was separated from her husband so it wasn't as if he was around the house. She said she was divorced and I didn't have a reason to doubt her."

"Well, to be fair, I suppose some people might not exactly consider themselves married when they're separated."

"It isn't exactly divorced, either. And since they were going to counseling and the husband believed they were trying to reconcile, that made her more married than not."

His tone was full of disgust, though Lindsey wasn't sure whether for Lori Springer's deception or for him-

self. In case it was for himself she said, "But you didn't know any of that."

"I knew it those last few weeks."

And that was what he condemned himself for, if his tone of voice was any indication.

"Finding out didn't end your relationship with her," Lindsey prompted.

"No, it didn't. Instead I tried to sway her into deciding to get a divorce." He shook his head. "I wooed and pursued her in a full-court press when I should have backed off."

Lindsey tried not to be envious of what that wooing and pursuing might have been. "Why?"

He gave a mirthless chuckle. "I was in love with her by then. Even though I didn't like what she'd done, I believed her when she said she'd done it because she was confused, that she hadn't set out to meet someone new, to be attracted to someone new, but that when it happened she'd thought she should explore it before making the decision of whether or not to go back to her husband. She said she'd figured I would never have had anything to do with her if I'd known she wasn't already divorced. She was right."

"You were an experiment." That slipped out. As did the derisive tone of Lindsey's dislike of this woman she'd never even met. "And by the time you found out she was still married you were up to your eyeballs in emotional involvement," she said. "So what happened?"

"The husband and I met each other one day when I dropped in on her unannounced. He was there. He hadn't known about me. I hadn't known about him. It was ugly. That was when I should have stepped out of the picture. I should have told her to look me up if

things didn't work out between them. But I didn't. I believed all her explanations, her claims to love me, her swearing she was just letting the husband down easily."

"But in the end it wasn't the husband she let down?"

"Three weeks after finding out about me, the husband, Marv, filed to divorce her and things changed. Fast. All of a sudden he was who she loved and wanted to be with."

"So she went back to him?"

"No. He wouldn't have her and when that happened she turned on me. Said it was my fault. I'd destroyed her chance for a happy marriage with the man she really loved."

Lindsey frowned. It was clear that Graham had bought into that blame to some degree and that he felt guilty.

"Her reaction seems a little extreme," Lindsey said tentatively because she wasn't sure just how defensive of the other woman he might still be. Or just how many feelings he might be harboring.

He looked directly at her for the first time since they'd been discussing this. "A *little* extreme? That's an understatement. But it opened my eyes to the kind of person she really was. I realized it wasn't only her marital status she'd hidden, but the dark side of her personality, too. Suddenly she wasn't the sweet, even-tempered, fun-loving woman I'd seen until then. She was someone who would sacrifice anything and anyone to get what she wanted, or even just to have what was only a passing need met. When push came to shove, Lori was all that mattered to Lori and other people were just the chess pieces she played."

Any thoughts Lindsey had about him carrying a torch for the other woman disappeared with that, for both his words and contemptuous tone stated clearly that he'd gotten over her. Lindsey knew she shouldn't feel so elated by that, but she did. "Does the dark side of her personality extend to abandoning her own children?"

He flinched slightly at that. "I don't know. I've thought about it. I'd like not to believe it. It was bad enough to have to face the fact that I'd fallen for a woman who would do the things she did. But to dump her own babies? That's even worse."

"And why would she do it?"

"She left here and moved to Santa Barbara, but a few days before Charlie and Kate appeared I heard through the grapevine that she'd recently reconnected with Marv. Rumor has it they hadn't seen each other in all that time, then met accidentally on vacation in Mexico and rekindled things. I was told she'd just now moved back to Denver, to the house she inherited from her grandparents. What I can't help wondering, given her penchant for keeping secrets, is what if she left here pregnant with the twins, had them and kept it from me out of spite and from Marv by virtue of just not having contact with him? But what if when she got together with Marv again she didn't want to bring that proof of our relationship into it and risk setting him off, so she left the kids with me?"

"Without letting him know she had two children?"

Graham shrugged. "If I hadn't found out on my own she might never have let me know she had a husband. Certainly she wouldn't have let him know about me. Besides, Marv Springer didn't strike me as a guy who would happily accept another man's children, especially not when those children are glaring reminders of

the affair his wife had when she claimed to be working on their marriage. He probably wouldn't take her back if that was part of the deal. And frankly, he's not a guy I would want anywhere near kids of mine."

"Understand that I'm only playing devil's advocate here, not defending this woman," Lindsey said. "But do you realize you're painting a picture of a person who could give birth to the twins, care for them for fifteen months and then just drop them like hot potatoes in order to have back her old husband?"

"Like I said, I don't want to believe it. But I do know she was not the maternal type. And she has the kind of money to pay other people to have cared for the twins the whole time, so it's possible she never really got attached to them. Actually, it was how she was raised. She said she could go months without even seeing her own parents when she was growing up, that she'd been left with nannies and governesses until she was old enough to go to boarding school, and then she only crossed paths with them on holidays. She said that sometimes she felt as if they wouldn't even recognize her if they came across her on the street instead of in their living room, where they knew who to expect. I felt sorry for her, but if she's Kate's and Charlie's mother, maybe that's how they were cared for, too. And maybe that's also why they don't cry for her."

Lindsey had to concede that that would also answer why they so easily accepted care from strangers. Maybe they'd learned to expect that, rather than any kind of motherly affection.

Lindsey was liking Lori Springer less and less.

"So you think she abandoned the twins to avoid anything that would have let her husband know the twins exist at all?"

He only raised an eyebrow in confirmation.

"I wish you would have told me all this from the start."

"I don't have good feelings for Lori or Marv Springer. But like I said, I'm not proud of whatever part I played in their marriage ultimately ending. I didn't want to throw a wrench into the works this time until I was sure there was a reason to."

So he hadn't been protecting the other woman, just trying not to cause trouble. Lindsey was feeling better and better. Even though she knew it shouldn't matter to her. "Was Lori Springer really so angry with you that she'd even keep news of your own kids from you?"

He let out another of those mirthless sighs disguised as a chuckle. "I couldn't explain it if I tried, but by the end she acted as if I'd single-handedly destroyed her marriage. She seemed to forget she and her husband were already separated by the time she met me. Hell, she seemed to forget everything but the fact that Marv found out about me and divorced her."

Again the memory made him shake his head. "I guess in a way it absolved her and her husband of whatever had gone wrong in their marriage to make someone outside of it the bad guy. All I know is that she did a complete about-face, said she hated me so much she couldn't stand the sight of me. It was pretty amazing. But it taught me a good lesson. I learned to beware of people in tumultuous times in their life because it's too easy to get sucked into the maelstrom, spit out and blamed for the damage, too. To answer your question—no, I don't think she'd have any qualms at all about leaving me in the dark about my own kids."

He'd built up quite a head of steam, which told her he definitely believed it.

Lindsey stood. "Well, no matter what's going on with her now, it's time I paid her a visit."

After a moment Graham nodded his agreement. "Annie will watch the kids while we're gone. They're ready for a nap, anyway."

He was right about that. Charlie and Kate were both heavy-lidded and headed for sleep. But the part of what he'd said that assumed he'd be going with Lindsey to question Lori Springer was something else again.

"I don't know if it's a good idea for you to come along."

"If she's done this I want to hear about it," he said forcefully, some of the anger in his last statement still alive and well. Then once more he jammed his hands through his hair, closing his eyes as if to gain some control. When he opened them he gave her a chagrined half smile.

"I'm sorry. I didn't mean to snap at you. It's just that I want to be there when she's confronted with this. I want to see her reaction. And I want some answers if it's true. I also don't want you going by yourself. She and Marv Springer are living there together again, and even though he's probably not home at this time of day, on the off chance that he might be, I don't want you facing him on your own. He's not a nice guy. He has a short fuse and a mean temper to go with it. Basically, he's a real horse's ass. I can't understand what she saw in him, but there's no way I'm letting you deal with him unless I'm there."

Graham's concern pleased her much more than it should have. But even so she couldn't let it go undebated. "This is what you hired me for, remember? Marv Springer wouldn't be the first hostile man I've faced."

Graham's expression relaxed into an engaging grin. "Okay, so you'll protect me," he teased. "But I'm still going."

IF LORI SPRINGER had, indeed, left Kate and Charlie in Graham's bedroom it wasn't because she was impressed with his house or the area it was in. Compared to the three-story white-brick minimansion Graham drove up to in one of Denver's older suburbs, his was a log cabin.

"The house that cod built—Lori's grandparents made a fortune selling fish, believe it or not. Then they invested in real estate when Denver was still a cow town and ended up with enough money for her parents and then her to just sit back and reap the benefits," he said as he pulled up to the iron gate that barred the driveway and pushed a button on an intercom.

An accented voice said, "Delivery?"

"Yes," Graham answered, then he shrugged at Lindsey. "I wasn't sure they'd let us in if they knew it was me out here, but that solved that."

"Whatever it takes."

The gates opened mechanically and he drove through, following the curve of the driveway to park directly in front of double doors that could have graced the entrance to a castle. They were open by the time Graham and Lindsey reached them, and there stood the woman in the picture she'd discovered—minus the diamonds but beautiful nonetheless.

"Oh my God, I was afraid that really was your car coming up. What are you doing here?" she demanded, barely glancing at Lindsey.

"We need to talk," Graham answered her, borrowing Lindsey's phrase.

"I don't have anything to say to you. And even if I did, Marv will be home any minute. He can't find you here."

"We'll keep it short. If you don't want him to see us, let us in and get this over with so we can leave before he comes home."

Lindsey looked on as the two of them stared eye-to-eye. The air between them was thick with discord, and since there seemed to be something of a stalemate going she decided to introduce herself.

She took a business card from her purse and handed it to the other woman. "There are some questions we'll have to ask you," she said authoritatively.

Lori Springer looked from the business card to Lindsey and then back to Graham. "What's going on?" she demanded.

"I might ask the same thing."

"After all this time fate put Marv and I back together to finally work out our differences. We have an appointment in an hour with a minister to arrange our wedding. *Nothing* you want to ask me is as important as that. And I won't have my second chance ruined by you."

She began to close the door in their faces but Lindsey stepped in to prevent that. "You're wasting time, Mrs. Springer. We can ask you the questions, or wait out here for your husband and ask him, if you'd rather. The choice is yours."

The look she shot Lindsey was venomous, but the threat worked. Instead of trying to force the door closed she opened it further. "There should be a law against this sort of harassment," she snapped as they went in.

But the entryway was as far as she was letting them go. When Lori had closed the door behind them she only turned to stare at them, not moving from that spot.

"Kate and Charlie," Graham said without preamble from where he and Lindsey stopped near a staircase that curved elegantly to the second floor.

Lori Springer's lovely face scrunched into a frown. "What?"

"Kate and Charlie," Lindsey repeated, handing the other woman the note that had come with them. "Twins, approximately fifteen months old. They were left in the middle of Graham's bedroom floor on Tuesday with that note."

Lori Springer barely gave it a glance before handing it back with a derisive snort of a laugh. "So what does this have to do with me?"

"That's what we're here to find out," Lindsey told her. "Are the babies yours?"

"You have to be kidding."

"Fifteen months plus nine—that means they were conceived just about the time we were ending our relationship," Graham said.

"And you think I'm their *mother?*"

"I'm asking," Graham said very seriously.

The blonde laughed but it sounded slightly hysterical. Lindsey wondered if that was because she was nervous about her husband catching them or because she was being confronted with what she'd done to her own children.

"I don't know what you're talking about. This whole thing is ridiculous. Just get out of here and leave me alone."

"I have two babies asleep at my house right this minute who aren't ridiculous at all. I want to know who

they are and where they came from and if they really are my kids."

She tossed a sneer in Lindsey's direction. "So you hired *her* to figure all of that out?"

"As a matter of fact."

"And she brought you here."

"Actually, I brought her here. When we discovered the twins and I have the same blood type."

The blond woman smirked. "Guess that makes them yours, then."

"Are you saying they are?" he asked, maintaining his patience in the face of her sarcasm.

"How would I know?" she answered, sounding coy.

"You'd know if you're their mother," Lindsey said.

"I'm nobody's *mother*." She again said the word as if it were obscene, and Lindsey wondered if she protested too much.

"So you're going on record that the babies aren't yours and Graham's?"

"Oh, please." She rolled her eyes. Then to Graham, "Will you get out of here and take her with you before you cause me any more trouble?"

"Are the twins yours and mine?" he repeated insistently.

"I do not have any kids," she said, exaggerating each syllable pointedly, glibly, nastily.

And because of that, Lindsey couldn't tell if it was the truth or not.

Apparently neither could Graham, because he said, "What if I guarantee Marv won't find out about them, that I'll keep the twins and never bother you again? Would you acknowledge that they're yours and mine then?"

Something turned her venomous again, whether the mention of her husband's name and the reminder that he'd be home soon, or the insinuation that she was lying. "Get out," she nearly shouted. "Get out now or I'll call the police and have you both arrested for trespassing."

Graham glared at her, but she only glared back, raising her chin to show she meant what she said and wouldn't be cowed by him.

Finally it was Lindsey who spoke, breaking the second stalemate. "Come on, Graham. We're not getting anywhere here."

Lori Springer's expression turned victorious.

For that reason Lindsey said what she otherwise would have waited to tell him after they'd left. "There are other ways to find out if she's the mother."

Victory turned to rage. The blond woman opened the door so forcefully she lost her grip on the handle and it banged into the wall. "Get out!"

Lindsey led the way to do just that, and no sooner had Graham followed her than the door crashed closed behind them.

"I know what you're thinking," he said as they headed down the front steps to his car. "I must have been out of my mind to ever have had anything to do with that witch."

Lindsey laughed lightly because that was exactly what had been going through her head.

"Before Marv filed for divorce and things fell apart I honestly never saw that side of her. In fact, I wouldn't have believed she was capable of it. She's like two different people—this one you just saw and the woman I met and fell in love with two and a half years ago. I

guess she missed her calling. She should have been an actress.''

''Or maybe she just has a few screws loose,'' Lindsey offered, hoping if the other woman had actually deserted her own children for the sake of a man who'd already divorced her once, that mental illness could be blamed rather than just plain vileness and selfishness.

But the conversation died as a black Mercedes pulled up behind Graham's red sports car and a man got out who was so handsome he was almost pretty.

He charged toward them.

Graham stood his ground where he'd just opened the passenger door for Lindsey, but she took a step in front of him, anyway, directly in the path of the man she had no doubt was Marv Springer.

Graham placed a hand on her arm and eased her back again, out of harm's way.

''What the hell are you doing here?'' Springer demanded, stopping just short of running into Graham.

Graham nodded in the direction of the house. ''Ask your wife.''

''She isn't my wife yet but she will be, so you have no business anywhere around her.''

The door to the house flew open again, and in a panicked voice Lori Springer called, ''Marv! Come in! I've just phoned for the police to deal with them!''

The Adonis stayed put, staring Graham down, his nostrils flaring in and out with the ferocity of an enraged animal.

Graham didn't budge, either, and finally, after Lori's third plea, Marv Springer relented.

''I'll get a restraining order to keep you away if I have to'' were his parting words.

"You won't have to" were Graham's as he put his hand on Lindsey's arm and urged her into the car.

"Charming people, the Springers," Lindsey joked when he'd joined her.

"Now you see why I didn't want you coming here alone."

She hated to tell him that the situation would probably have been much less volatile had he not been with her.

"So, what do you think?" he asked as he drove out the gates and headed for the highway back to Evergreen.

"What do *you* think?"

"That she's lying. That she pretended not to know what we were talking about to cover her tracks."

"That's possible," Lindsey allowed. "If she would dump her babies, anything is possible."

"But you weren't convinced?"

"Not either way—not that she is the mother, not that she isn't."

"Where do we go from here then?" he asked.

"You go home to the twins, and I go home to my telephone."

"To do what?"

"First to call my brother Logan. He's a cop, which comes in handy when I want to check for prior arrests or complaints."

Graham glanced over at her. "For the Springers?"

"You were right—he's a hothead. And she's not too even-tempered herself. I'm just curious about the forms that might have taken in the past. Then I'll start calling hospitals and the records department in Santa Barbara to see if I can turn up something that way."

He smiled at her. "So you weren't bluffing when you said there were other ways to find out if she's Kate's and Charlie's mother. I thought you might be." He checked the road and then glanced back at her. "And then what do you have planned for later? A hot Friday night on the town?"

A TV dinner and some closet organizing. But she wasn't going to admit that. "Just a quiet evening."

He looked at her out of the corner of his eye. "Alone?"

"Mmm."

"Great. Then how about the twins and I pick you up at six for a picnic in a park somewhere? I think they're getting tired of being cooped up. I know I am. And I thought we should take advantage of this beautiful Indian summer weather. I'll bet they'll love swings and teeter-totters and slides, and I'll pack all the food. What do you say?"

No—that was what every bit of common sense told her to say. He was asking her out on a date. All dates with clients were off-limits, at least the limits she'd set for herself. Certainly dates with clients she found much too appealing for her own good, at a time when she was much too vulnerable, were doubly off-limits. And this particular client happened to have two adorable kids she was inordinately susceptible to just when she was needing to wean herself from kids altogether. Strike three.

No, no, no.

But somehow when she opened her mouth to say it, out came "That sounds like fun."

And then he grinned over at her as if he'd been worried she might turn him down and was very pleasantly surprised, and she really was sunk.

Deep into the depths of those electric blue eyes of his.

Because off-limits or not, common sense or not, vulnerable or not, there was nothing she could think of at that moment that she'd rather do than spend an evening picnicking in the park with him.

And no way she could deny herself.

TRUE TO HIS WORD, Graham pulled up in front of Lindsey's small house at six on the dot that evening.

She was watching for him from the living room window when he stopped the rental car with her two child carriers full of babies in the back seat.

Something about that first sight of him in a family sedan complete with family made her smile. He just didn't seem to fit the picture even though the satisfied expression on his face let her know he was enjoying the novelty.

She didn't wait for him to come to the door but rushed out so he wouldn't have to either leave the twins alone in the car or unload them to come get her.

Besides, she'd been dreading the thought since leaving him at home in Evergreen that he might bring the babies into her house. She honestly didn't think she could face having them on her territory. Tiny feet pattering on the hardwood floors, baby voices echoing in the too-empty rooms, baby scents infusing the air...

No, it had taken her too long to clear the place of reminders. She didn't need Kate and Charlie here to bring some of them back.

"You look very picnicky," Graham greeted her as she met him near the car. His gaze did a quick dash downward from her white shirt to the cutoffs that had replaced the blue jeans she'd worn earlier and back again to her face. "Very nice," he murmured appreciatively, as if she'd been dressed in her finest.

It made Lindsey laugh and return the compliment with just a hint of teasing, though he did look very fine in a tennis shirt and shorts. Then she said, "There's a park just north of here unless you had some place else in mind."

"Just tell me where," he answered, sweeping an arm out for her to get in the car ahead of him.

And for some reason, as she did Lindsey had the sense he was checking her out from behind the same way he'd checked her out from the front. But since more than once she'd enjoyed the sight of his great derriere, she guessed she couldn't fault him.

"Mmm, you smell good, too," he said as he opened the car door for her and she stepped in front of him to get in.

He was no slouch in the after-shave department, either, but she only said, "Thanks," and fought a secret thrill that he'd noticed and liked the perfume she'd argued with herself about using tonight.

The five-minute drive to the park was taken up with directions, but once they'd arrived and unloaded the car of babies and picnic gear Graham asked if her phone calls in the afternoon had turned up anything.

"A big zero," she told him as they set a blanket out and put Kate and Charlie in the center of it. "No one I spoke to came across a birth certificate with Lori Springer as the mother. But that doesn't necessarily mean anything. She could have used a different name. Or she could have had the babies somewhere else. We're only assuming she was in Santa Barbara at the time."

"But if she wasn't, she could have been anywhere in the world," he said as he began breaking peanut-butter-and-jelly sandwiches into tiny pieces for the twins.

"Why don't you contact whoever it was who told you the rumors about how she reconnected with her ex, where she'd been living, all of that. Find out all you can about anyplace she might have lived or vacationed during the last fifteen months, any names of people she might have been associated with, anything. The smallest detail could be something we could follow up on. I can contact your source but usually grapevines function better on friendly terms than with strangers."

"I'll try, but the end of the grapevine I heard it from isn't likely to know much more."

For their dinner he'd brought an antipasto fit for Italian kings, and as they each began to sample it, Lindsey said, "I also think we should look into some other possibilities."

He was chewing, and until he finished he raised his eyebrows at her. Then he said, "Such as?"

"I think we should explore your family."

"My family," he repeated, as if the suggestion confused him.

"The next most likely connection to the blood type would be from someone related to you, someone else in your family who has AB-negative and passed it along to the twins. Could be that they decided good-old distant-cousin Graham could provide for their kids better than they could and christened you daddy."

He thought about that. "I don't have many relatives. My family was small to begin with and I've lost the closest ones over the years. In fact, I think that contributed to my being so susceptible to Lori Springer. My father had passed away not long before that and I was feeling pretty alone." He shook his head dubiously. "I don't know, it seems a lot more likely that Kate and Charlie are mine."

"But we can't lose sight of the fact that Lori Springer denied it, and we haven't turned up anything solid to support it."

"The note," he reminded.

"Still, I don't think we should ignore some other possibilities. You did hire me to do this right, didn't you?"

But he didn't answer that.

They were both sitting Indian fashion not far from the babies, the plate of meats and cheeses between them on the blanket. Kate suddenly got up and plopped down on Graham's lap to help herself to one of the olives in the center of the tray.

Lindsey watched as the big man took it from her, broke it in half and fed it to her so she wouldn't choke by eating the whole thing at once. The affection and tender care he offered were very endearing. She knew he believed the kids were his. But she also knew she had to do all she could to find out if that was true.

"Okay," he finally said, sounding as if he were just humoring her, "I'll take you on a climb through my family tree. But not tonight. This is Friday, we're out for a picnic and you've done enough work. Right now I want you to close up shop and just relax."

It was a direct order but delivered with a smile that was so magnetic, for a moment Lindsey got stuck on it.

Then Charlie came to her and perched his diapered rear end on her knee as if it were a milking stool so he could see what his sister had come to share. He chose a tightly rolled slice of ham for himself.

Lindsey glanced from the little boy, to Kate, to Graham, knowing that somewhere along the way tonight she'd lost even the slightest resistance to the three of them, and she realized she might as well roll with it.

"Tomorrow, then," she answered as if she really still had a grip on things when in reality all her willpower was drowned by the pure pleasure of being a part of this familylike group.

"Fine. Tomorrow," Graham assured. "But for the rest of tonight just enjoy yourself."

"It's been a long time since I've done that," she said with a wry laugh, though it wasn't exactly true because she'd been enjoying herself a lot since meeting this man. It had just been disguised as work.

"Then I guess we'd better remind you how to let down your hair. What do you say we start with the swings?" he said, but there was such a devilish glint in those gorgeous eyes of his that it infused the suggestion with innuendo.

And to her surprise, Lindsey was all set to banter back. To flirt. Outrageously.

She curbed the urge in a hurry.

He grinned at her, as if he suspected she'd chickened out of a comeback but only stood with Kate in one arm and reached the other down to help Lindsey up. "Come on, Ms. Detective. A good time is about to be had by all."

"Promises, promises." Okay, so that slipped out on a seductive note of its own. But suddenly Lindsey didn't care anymore. It was as if she'd been squeezed tight by the restrictions of sad emotions for long enough and she wanted to let loose a little, to be as carefree as a kid. And where better to do it than in this play park, with two babies as an excuse and an attractive, intelligent man who deserved the credit for making her feel alive again?

She took his hand, trying not to be so aware of the contact that sent charges of electricity all the way up her

arm at just his simple touch, and stood with Charlie riding her hip. "Okay, let's do it."

His expression lit up and she could tell he was resisting a comeback of his own—no doubt lascivious. But instead of saying anything, he kept hold of her hand and headed for the sandy playground area not far away.

And that was how the rest of the evening went.

Graham flirted with her and Lindsey did her fair share of flirting back. He never missed a chance to touch her—to take her hand or arm, to squeeze her shoulders, to clasp the back of her neck.

And somehow it seemed perfectly natural.

So natural that Lindsey found herself leaning into each contact and even initiating some of her own, reaching out to him, nudging his side when she'd bested him at speed diapering, even brushing sand out of his hair when Charlie threw some there.

For Kate and Charlie's part, they loved the swings and teeter-totter, shrieked on the merry-go-round and no sooner reached the bottom of the slide than they toddled around to go again—always on Lindsey's lap.

Not that she minded. On the contrary, it gave her an excuse to slip through the tunnel at the top, which was too small for Graham, and swoosh down the hilly slide hanging onto a pudgy baby whose tiny sounds of delight were like bits of pure sunshine.

By the time it got dark the babies were slaphappy tired and Lindsey was worn out, too. Only Graham seemed unfazed.

As they each carried a baby away from the playground, he reached an arm around Lindsey's shoulders and pulled her in close to his side, pressing a quick kiss to her hair as if that, too, was an everyday occurrence.

"This was better than work, wasn't it?" he asked in a near whisper, so close to her ear she felt the warmth of his breath.

"I had a really good time," she admitted.

"It isn't how I usually spend first dates, though, I have to tell you," he confessed as they took the weary babies to the car and settled them snugly into their seats before going for the picnic things still on the grass nearby.

"No, I would guess wining and dining are more your norm," she teased him with a sidelong glance.

"Are you going to give me a chance to do that when this is all over with?"

Lindsey stopped midway in reloading the wicker basket he'd brought and then forced herself to go on so he wouldn't see how unnerving that question was to her. She decided to make light of it. "Better see how it ends. You may not like the answers I come up with and might want to shoot the messenger rather than wine and dine her."

"I don't think so," he said with conviction emphasized by the firm slam of the trunk once they'd set everything inside it. "No, I don't think so at all," he repeated on his way around the car to hold the passenger door open for her.

They didn't say much on the short drive back to Lindsey's house, but she was very aware of Graham, just the same. Of the bulge of his biceps and the sinews of his forearms below the sleeves of his shirt. Of his big, capable hands on the steering wheel. Of the way his hair waved against his nape. Of those broad shoulders pressed into the seat. Of the curve of his hips into thighs that were thick, strong, speckled with hair and spread far apart...

"Here we are," he said as he pulled into her driveway, surprising her since she'd been more interested in him than in the trip to her house.

"You don't have to get out. Just take the twins home," she said in a rush to recover her wandering thoughts.

He turned off the engine, anyway, nodding toward the babies. "They're already sleeping. They won't miss me," he assured, getting out of the car and coming around to her side.

She didn't wait for him to open her door, though, and was just closing it when he reached her.

He kept a little distance from her as they went up the walk to her front porch, and she had to admit to herself that she missed the touch he'd shared through the evening.

"Now this part of the deal is not great," he said as they climbed the three steps into the glow of the porch light.

"What part of what deal?"

"Kate and Charlie. Ordinarily I'd be hoping for an invitation in for a nightcap to prolong this evening a little, but now that can't happen."

"Mmm" was all Lindsey said, thinking it was probably a good thing, because otherwise inviting him in was just what she might do.

She pulled her keys out of her purse, but before she could get them in the door he took them from her and unlocked it for her, pushing it open.

"Thanks," she said, hating that most of her voice had deserted her and it came out a soft, breathy sound. She cleared her throat and tried again. "And thanks for the picnic, for the whole evening."

This time "Mmm" was all he said, staring down at her, studying her as if he were reading something in her eyes.

And Lindsey stared back, lost in that handsome, chiseled face, knowing she should just say good-night and go in but held there by something in the air between them.

He bent to her then, capturing her mouth with his in a courting kiss that lasted only a few moments before his arms wrapped her and he drew her up, closer, higher, holding her against the solidness of his big body, cradling the back of her head in one hand while the other pressed against her spine.

His lips parted and so did hers, as if following an irresistible lead.

Lindsey couldn't help drifting away on it, letting her head rest in his palm, accepting the glory of his warm, masculine mouth, feeling her breasts give way to the hardness of his chest, learning the hills and hollows of his broad back with her hands splayed against it even though she didn't remember how they'd got there in the first place.

And all she could think was that she wished it could go on forever. That this kiss could run into another and another. Deeper and deeper. That tongues might explore and learn. That she could reach under his shirt and know the feel of his bare skin...

She wanted so much more of him that it began to scare her. And that fear brought to mind all the reasons why he was off-limits to her, reminding her that this man—handsome, charming, warm, funny, fun—just might be the same kind of package that had caused her so much pain and heartache in the past.

She ended the kiss, pulling away as far as he'd let her go, which wasn't very far at all. "This isn't a good idea," she murmured as forcefully as she could.

"Felt pretty good," he countered with a small smile.

"I don't...do this...with clients," she managed, struggling to find the right words without having to delve too deeply into all the reasons why it shouldn't be happening.

"I'm glad to know that," he said, that smile stretching wider. "I'd hate to think it was par for the course."

"No, I mean—"

"I know what you mean." He kissed her again and then let her go. "But sometimes things we don't usually do, things we don't plan, happen anyway."

"We don't need to let them."

"Don't we?" he asked, leaving the question to hang in the air for her to take with her, to think about.

Then he leaned and kissed her one more time on the lips and once on the tip of her nose. "I'll see you tomorrow, Lindsey," he said, turning and going down the walk to his car.

She watched him the whole way, wishing he wasn't leaving, knowing it was a good thing he was and wondering all over again if she should have taken this case in the first place.

Because he was right, it might be unplanned, but something was happening between them.

And she didn't seem capable of stopping it.

Off-limits or not.

Chapter Five

"All this great food and you won't stay long enough to eat any of it?" Lindsey's brother Quinn said when she joined him, his fiancée Cara and Logan at Simms Landing the next day while the three of them had brunch.

"Can't," Lindsey said, accepting only a cup of coffee. "I'm on my way to the client's house. I just stopped to say hello and hear what Logan found out about the Springers."

Cara came back from the buffet table just then, and the minute she was in her chair Quinn's arm went across the back of it as if to seal her into their own private space.

Lindsey watched Cara scoot the seat nearer to him and pop a strawberry into his mouth, all without either of them seeming to be conscious of what they were doing. They were truly two halves instinctively forming a whole, each appearing more happy, more content, more complete when they were together.

A jolt of jealousy hit Lindsey like a downed power line. And besides that jealousy, she wasn't happy to realize that when she put herself in that scenario, the man she shared it with in her mind was Graham.

But after spending hours the night before and this morning reminding herself of all the reasons why kisses like the past evening's and a relationship with him could not happen, she fled from the image in her head and focused on Logan.

"So," she said too brightly, too forcefully, "did you run the Springers for priors?"

"It's probably the last time I'll be able to do it for you, but yes, I did," he answered.

That distracted Lindsey from her case, her jealousy of what her other brother had found with Cara and even from thoughts of Graham. For the moment, anyway. "You tendered your resignation from the police force," she guessed in a much more subdued tone because she knew how difficult that choice was for Logan.

"By this time next week we'll have a new partner," Quinn said, clearly trying to be upbeat. "We'll be Strummel, Strummel and Strummel of Strummel Investigations."

Lindsey bent over and gave Logan a hug. "I'm sorry you had to make this decision but I'm glad you'll be working with us."

"Thanks," he said. But he didn't seem to want to talk anymore about it. Instead he cleared his throat and addressed what she'd asked before. "The Springers, now, they're an interesting couple."

Lindsey stole a minimuffin from Logan's plate and ate it while he filled her in.

"I don't know anything about Marv Springer except what I read in the reports, but Lori I happen to be familiar with myself. I just couldn't tell you when you called. I was at my desk with listening ears close by."

Lindsey was surprised. "Did you meet her when you were doing debutante duty?"

"A speeding ticket. She tracked me down at the station a few days after I'd issued it to her and then showed up several times when my shift was ending, wanting to have coffee, or dinner. Basically she tried to seduce me." He grinned wryly and shook his head. "She almost made it, too."

"Why didn't she?"

"I happened to find out—purely by accident—that she was not the nice lady she appeared to be and that Marv Springer wasn't her brother the way she'd told me he was."

So Graham wasn't the only one she'd lied to.

"Anyway," Logan continued, "the Springers could be the poster couple for domestic discord. There's a whole string of reports of disturbances and violations of restraining orders—on both sides. There are as many against her as against the husband. Although there's nothing recent. The reports end about two years ago."

"She left town," Lindsey supplied. "Did anything ever come of the arrests?"

"The charges were always dropped. Apparently they'd kiss and make up before getting to court. Probably because one of them is as bad as the other. She's gone after him with broken bottles, he's backhanded her in front of witnesses, they've trashed each others' houses when they've lived apart, totaled expensive automobiles as if they were amusement-park bumper cars, slashed tires, set fire to front lawns, broken windows, you name it. And anybody who gets in the line of fire goes down, too."

"Has anyone else gone through with charges against either of them?" she asked.

Logan rubbed his thumb and fingertips together. "Money, honey. Big settlements get the charges dropped."

"Any mention in the later reports of her being pregnant?"

"No, but only private physicians were used so there wasn't a lot of medical information available."

"From what you know of Lori Springer yourself, did she strike you as a woman who could abandon her own kids and then deny they were hers at all?"

"Hey, I wouldn't put anything past her. Or him, either, for that matter, which is why I'd steer clear of them both, if you can."

Lindsey made a muscle and joked, "Don't worry about me. I'm in great shape."

"As a matter of fact," Cara mentioned, "you do look much better than I've seen you. Your cheeks are rosy and your eyes are bright. Working must agree with you."

"Or her client does," Logan offered, supplying a tasty tidbit of gossip.

Quinn frowned worriedly at her. "You aren't getting personally involved with him, are you? Not so soon after your divorce? You know that's just asking for trouble."

"Who would know better than me?" she answered. She stood, before her brothers could delve deeper into the subject. "Gotta go. Thanks for the information," she said to Logan, squeezing his shoulder. "I'll see everybody later."

But as she made her way out of the restaurant to her car and headed for Evergreen, she had to admit to herself that while, yes, working again definitely agreed with

her, so did Graham Dunn. Everything about him. About being with him.

Not that that was a good thing because it wasn't.

Not when he was a client.

Not when he potentially came complete with kids.

Not when she was just coming off a disastrous relationship of her own.

No, no matter how much being with him agreed with her, she was absolutely clear about all the reasons why she really needed to keep what was happening between them under control.

Which was just what she was going to do.

Unfortunately, what she wasn't absolutely clear about was how she was going to do it.

GRAHAM WAS TALKING on a cordless phone when he answered the front door at his house a while later. He motioned Lindsey in and closed it behind her.

"Here's how it is, Lori," she heard him say firmly but without anger into the telephone. "Either you come here or I'll bring them there. So which will it be?"

Lindsey shot him a look, wondering what he was doing.

He silently mouthed "It's okay" and went back to listening to whatever Lori Springer was saying on the other end.

He was wearing a pair of jeans Lindsey was getting used to seeing him in and a red-and-black-checked rugby shirt with a tan collar. But he hadn't shaved yet today, even though it was nearly one o'clock, and his hair was slightly mussed.

On anyone else it might be unattractive, but on him it seemed so sexy he could have marketed it.

Then he said into the phone, "All right. But if you don't show up, expect me on your doorstep. Even if I have to track you to Timbuktu." He pushed the button to disconnect the call and jammed down the antenna.

"What was all of that?" Lindsey asked, glad to be distracted from assessing his appearance.

"I got to thinking that it might be enlightening to get the twins face-to-face with Lori. I have no doubt she could hide any reaction to them, but if she's their mother maybe they'll respond to her."

Lindsey conceded that the idea had some merit. "I take it from your threat to take them to her place that she wasn't cooperative."

"She's holding hard to the claim that the kids aren't hers. But *threat* is such an ugly word. Let's just say it took some persuading to override her lack of enthusiasm," he said with a devilish smile. "She'll be here late this afternoon."

"With or without Marv?"

"Without. She doesn't want him knowing any of what's going on. Interesting, isn't it? If the kids aren't hers, why not just tell him why I've contacted her and that I'm barking up the wrong tree thinking that she's Kate and Charlie's mother?"

"Maybe she just doesn't want to set him off," Lindsey suggested, going on to relay what Logan had said about the happy couple.

"I'd like to say I'm shocked, but I'm not. I've seen both Lori's and Marv's tempers," he said when she'd finished. "But it is nice to know she duped your brother for a while, too. I'd hate to think I was the only person who fell for her phony charms."

"How about your grapevine source? Did you turn up anything there?"

He shook his head. "Nothing we didn't already know. You did a much better job. I guess that's why you're the pro and I'm the rank amateur."

Jokingly, she breathed on her fingernails and polished them against the shoulder of her red camp shirt. But then she got right back to business. "So. I thought we were going to concentrate on a direction other than the Springers today?"

"My family tree," he confirmed. "Sure. I'll tell you the whole short story. But would you mind if I stand next to a razor first? The twins are demolishing the kitchen cupboards. You can see how good they are at it while I finish what I started at seven this morning, believe it or not."

So the two tiny tots were still getting the best of the big mountain man. Lindsey couldn't help smiling at that. But she hedged just the same about watching them herself. She'd known in advance of coming here that she would be extravulnerable to them today and had hoped to avoid too much contact. "Isn't Annie coming in?" she asked.

"Soon. She's been great about working extra and helping out. I knew she was a gem before, but she's worth her weight in gold right now." His eyebrows rose at her. "I can put off shaving until she gets here if you don't want to keep an eye on the twins for some reason."

It seemed so silly when he said it out loud that she couldn't stick with her feeble attempt to keep her distance. "No, that's okay. Go ahead."

He didn't need more encouragement than that. "Won't take me a minute," he said. And then he pecked a familiar kiss on her cheek, taking her off guard before he disappeared down the adjoining hallway.

Lindsey had to wait out the tingling that the kiss rained all through her, and by the time she had remembered she should have chastised him for it, he was long gone and it was too late.

But she really should have let him know not to do that.

She liked it altogether too much....

The sound of metal clattering on ceramic tile came from the kitchen, reminding her where she was supposed to be, and she headed there.

Demolishing the cupboards was just what the twins were doing, she discovered.

The door to every one they could reach was open and the contents spilled onto the floor as if they were searching for something.

"All the toys Graham bought you guys and this is what you want to play with?"

Both babies noticed her then. Charlie grinned with delight, and Kate patted the tile beside her and said, "Sit," so endearingly that Lindsey's resistance melted on the spot.

"I shouldn't," she said as she did. "I'm headed for a bad day tomorrow and playing with you two is only going to make it worse."

But she ended up cross-legged between them, anyway.

"See?" Charlie asked, displaying a small saucepan before he put it on Kate's head like a hat.

The little girl sat up straighter and preened as if it were an Easter bonnet, waiting for Lindsey's approval.

"Very nice," she said with a laugh. "Think we could put some of this stuff back *in* the cupboard?"

"No," Kate answered, never one to have trouble making up her mind.

Lindsey replaced a few pans in spite of the baby's orders, but that set Charlie off.

"Mine!" he told her in no uncertain terms, crawling into the cupboard to retrieve a double boiler.

But on the way back out he misjudged the distance and came up too soon, bumping his head hard on the upper shelf.

"Ooh—" Lindsey's instincts took over and she reached for him, pulling him onto her lap while he caught his breath and then wailed. "Poor Charlie. That hurt, didn't it?" she cooed, holding him close and rocking back and forth to soothe him.

She was sorry he'd hurt himself, but it felt so good to have him in her arms, to have his pudgy little body snuggling up to her, that she couldn't resist curling her shoulders around him and closing her eyes.

That was a mistake.

Time suddenly turned backward in her mind, and she was in another place not so long ago, not so far away, holding another little boy....

She absorbed the feel of that baby in her arms as if it might stay with her, as if she might be able to stock up on it to take out later, in small bits, to savor after tomorrow when she'd really need it....

"What happened?" Graham's voice was anxious, coming from just above her.

She opened her eyes and raised them up the long length of her client, fighting her way back to the present. "I made the mistake of putting some stuff away. Bobby crawled in to get it and bumped his head."

"Bobby?"

Had she really said that? Oh, Lord.

"Charlie! I meant Charlie," she amended in a rush.

Graham hunkered down on his heels, the look of concern on his handsome face as much for her as the baby. "Is everything okay?"

Charlie's crying had settled down with the appearance of Graham, not to mention the comfort of two baby fingers in the mouth. Lindsey purposely overlooked the part of Graham's curiosity that included her and glanced down at the top of the baby's head where it rested against her breasts.

"He's fine. It didn't even break the skin. He'll probably have a little lump but that's all." And she managed to sound perfectly okay herself. Quite a feat at that moment.

Graham first checked out Charlie's head, then his gaze settled on Lindsey much the same way. But if he saw anything that left him wondering if she was all right, it didn't show.

Lindsey drank in the nearness of him to ground herself. His hair was combed casually to one side, teasing his temple, his face was clean shaven and smelled wonderful, and something about his strong presence helped chase away the demons.

He sat on the floor then, facing her, closed a cupboard door and leaned against it. "You may be a better detective than I am, but I leave you alone with a couple of kids and look what happens," he teased.

"Hey, we can't all be good at everything," she joked, appreciating his effort to lighten the mood.

Kate went to him and tried the saucepan hat on his head. It didn't fit but he let her set it there, anyway, and Lindsey liked that he didn't mind having his hair messed up or looking pretty silly—just one more thing on the growing list of what she appreciated about this man.

"Family connections," she prompted to get her mind off him.

"Not a lot to tell, but there is a skeleton in the closet." He was obviously enjoying intriguing her.

"Inbreeding? That would explain a lot." It was her turn to tease him again.

He laughed. "No, not quite that bad."

"What then?"

"If the AB-negative blood didn't come directly from me, it has to be from my mother's side of the family. My father had heart surgery not long before he died, and they couldn't use my blood when they needed it because it was the wrong kind."

"Okay, so we concentrate on your mother's side. Is that where the skeleton is?"

"I'm afraid so. And because of it, anything to do with my mother's family may not be easy to check out. My parents were divorced when I was a little kid—about four—and I only saw her once after that."

"How come?"

"I guess because she didn't want to see me. She'd had an affair and when she found out she was pregnant by the other man, she left."

He didn't say that as if it carried any pain with it anymore, but then after thirty-odd years, she supposed he'd dealt with whatever his feelings about his mother were.

He went on. "The one time I saw her was a year later, the first week of kindergarten. She showed up at the school and walked home with me—well, not all the way home, but up to the block just before. And that was the last I ever saw of her. About a month later we heard she died in a car accident."

There was some sadness tingeing that last part, but
Lindsey could tell it was old sadness. Still, she gave him
a moment before going on, and he used it to pull Kate
onto his lap.

"What about the baby she was carrying when she left
your father?" Lindsey finally asked.

"I don't know. She didn't say anything about it that
day I saw her. And if my father knew anything, he never
said it to me. My mother or anything to do with her
wasn't a subject he discussed. In fact, beyond telling me
she'd been killed, there was next to nothing else he ever
said about her."

"You're sure it was a full year between when she left
and when you saw her again?"

"She left on Labor Day. I can't tell you how I remember that, being as small as I was, but I do. And
school starts after Labor Day, so it had to be a year
later."

"Then more than likely she had the baby during that
time."

"Sure. Abortion wasn't legal then. Unless she lost it
naturally, she must have. Which means I probably have
a half brother or half sister out there somewhere."

"You've never considered looking for him or her?"

"No, not really."

"Why is that?"

He shrugged. "Oh, I don't know, Lindsey. Loyalty,
I guess."

"To your father?"

He nodded. "My father was not a man to show
emotion. He never in his life told me he loved me, or
praised me for anything, or thanked me for a gift or
something I did for him. In fact, there were times
growing up when I thought that it was no wonder my

mother turned to someone else because he could be so remote, so tough to connect with. Given that, you can imagine what it was like to lie in my bed and hear him cry after she left. *Cry.* My father, of all people." Graham shook his head as if he still found it difficult to believe, and Lindsey watched his face tighten before he buried it in the top of Kate's head.

But the little girl wasn't having any of that and wiggled out of his lap.

Then he went on. "But even for all his coldness, my father was good to me. He worked hard to take care of me. He stuck with me, and my mother didn't. For me to have dug up the child who had come from her affair would have hurt him all over again. And by the time I was an adult and had the means, I just didn't see the point in causing that."

"You know, though, that the twins could have some connection to that half sibling," Lindsey said.

He met her eyes with his oh-so-blue ones. "I think it's farfetched. More than likely they're mine. But if for no other reason than to cancel the possibility, I guess we'd better go ahead and look into it."

"Do you know anything at all about him or her? Or the name of the man your mother was involved with?"

"No, to all of that. I don't have the foggiest idea. And there was nothing in anything my father left that might have given us a clue or I would have come across it when he died."

"How about a friend or relative of your mother's who might know? Do you remember anyone like that?"

"We're talking a long time ago," he said, pausing to think about it. Then something dawned on him. "I seem to recall an uncle—Uncle Howard. I went to his house once, in downtown Denver. My mother took me

there on a bus. It was a great adventure for me. But if memory serves, he seemed a lot older than my mother. Maybe he was her uncle."

"Do you remember his last name?"

Graham shook his head. "Unless it was the same as my mother's maiden name—Douglas. He could have been Howard Douglas."

"Let's see if he's in the phone book."

Graham gave her a lopsided smile. "Is that how real investigators do it? They look in the phone book?"

"Whatever works. It's always a good place to start."

He got to his feet and left the kitchen for a moment, coming back with the white pages. "I'll be surprised if he's still alive. He was old over thirty years ago."

"A child's perception of things isn't always accurate," Lindsey said as she searched for his uncle's name. But even she was surprised when she found the listing. "There is a Douglas, Howard G.—and at an address that would put him in the heart of downtown, just off Spear Boulevard. If this is the same person you remember, maybe the *G* is for Graham and you were named for him."

"My father never said that, but then he wouldn't have. And at this point, anything is possible. Shall we call him?"

"I'd rather meet him. And it wouldn't hurt for you to come along and see if he looks familiar to you."

As if on cue, the back door opened just then and Annie called, "Yoo-hoo, Graham, it's me."

"Looks like I'll have a sitter," he said. "Unless of course you were planning to keep Charlie glued to you forever."

Don't tempt me, she thought.

Actually, the feel of the little boy in her lap was so right she'd forgotten he was even there, and he was snuggled in so comfortably she hated to disturb him.

Graham must have realized the two of them weren't going to part voluntarily because he went to the pantry and got a box of teething biscuits.

And that was all it took to lure the baby away.

"Thrown over for a cookie," Lindsey joked to hide the emptiness she felt once again.

"Come on," Graham urged. "Let's play detective and I'll see what I can do to make it up to you later."

But the tone in his voice wasn't promising anything as innocent as holding a little boy in her lap.

HOWARD DOUGLAS WAS, indeed, Graham's uncle, and more than that, the old man recognized him within a few moments of opening the door to Graham and Lindsey.

"My niece's boy. I know who you are," he said to Graham's introduction. "Read an article 'bout you a few months back and remember what you looked like in the pictures in it. I may be eighty-seven but I'm all right up here." He poked his temple with a bony index finger. "Come on in."

They followed him into a postage-stamp-size house and sat on the faded sofa he directed them to, while he turned the sound down on a black-and-white television whose picture was more snow than program and then settled into a brown recliner himself.

There wasn't any family resemblance between Howard Douglas and Graham that Lindsey could see. The old man had a triangular-shaped head, and what hair he had left was shaved in a buzz cut that only exaggerated his enormous ears. Lindsey guessed that he'd never been

a large man, but now he was downright scrawny, as if there were only fragile bones inside his dress trousers, plaid flannel shirt and green cardigan sweater.

"Got the magazine right here, more'n likely," he said, looking through a stack beside his chair, all of the same weekly publication in which Lindsey had discovered the picture of Graham and Lori Springer. "It was really something to read my magazine the same as I always do and all of a sudden see somebody I knew. Didn't think I was related to any celebrities. And now here you are, sittin' in my living room when I never thought I'd see you again at all." He found the issue he was looking for and held it up, slapping it with the back of his other hand. "This one!"

"We'd like to ask you some questions, if that would be okay, Mr. Douglas," Lindsey began.

He set the magazine back where it had come from, apparently concerned that the correct numerical order be kept and that the stack be lined up perfectly. "'Bout what?"

"The child Graham's mother was pregnant with when she left Graham and his father. Was that child born before she was killed?"

He nodded. "Charmayne."

Lindsey asked him to spell it and wrote it on her tablet.

"Does she live in Denver by any chance?" Graham asked.

"Oh, no, she moved to Colorado Springs 'bout fifteen years ago. Got married young and had a baby of her own lickety-split. Called her Francine, after your mother. Guess she'd be your half niece, Francine would. Then Charmayne's husband got work in the Springs and they left. Francine was about two or three,

so that'd make her seventeen or so now. She used to like to crawl up in my lap because I gave her lemon drops."

"Is that where Charmayne and her family are now— Colorado Springs?" This from Lindsey.

The old man shrugged but his shoulders were so slight they barely raised the clothes that covered them. "Couldn't say. Never heard from her after she moved."

"What would Charmayne's last name be?" Lindsey again.

"Oh, now let me think 'bout that. I had a way of remembering...." He wrinkled up his already-wrinkled brow even more with the effort, closing his eyes to concentrate. "It was those peanuts...Planter! That was it. She was Charmayne Planter. Her husband's name was Norris." He opened his eyes and beamed proudly at his recollection.

Lindsey wrote it all down. "Any chance you might have an old Christmas card or letter, something that had her address in Colorado Springs?"

"No room 'round here to keep things like that for all this time."

"What about Charmayne's father? What was his name?"

"Porter. William Porter. But he won't be able to help you out. He passed on, oh, a good ten years ago."

"Charmayne would have been...twenty-five," Graham said as if he were thinking out loud, and Lindsey had the sense he was regretting that he hadn't known his half sister at a time when she might have appreciated having a brother.

"What about William Porter—did he remarry after Graham's mother died? Did he have more children?"

"No, just Charmayne."

"Is there anyone else you can think of who might have information about her, especially if she's left Colorado Springs? It's important that we locate her."

He puckered up the corners of his mouth as he thought about that but then shook his head and apologized. "Can't think of anybody."

"Just one more thing, Mr. Douglas. Have you heard anything at all about twins being born in your family—even in your remote family—a little over a year ago?"

"Don't have any remote family."

"So you don't know about a baby boy and girl named Charlie and Kate?"

His white brows arched up and he shook his head. "Can't say that I do. Should I?"

"No. We just needed to know if you had." Lindsey took one of her business cards out of her purse to give to him, making her usual end-of-interview request for a call if he remembered something else.

But Graham didn't seem inclined to leave.

"Is there anything we can do for you? Anything you need?" he asked his uncle.

Howard shooed the idea with the flip of a hand. "I'm all right. I have good friends and neighbors who help out since I had to stop driving."

"What about money?"

"I get by."

"Food?"

"I'm fine."

"Would it be okay if I keep in touch? Maybe we could take in a ball game, get a steak . . ."

The old guy grinned and in that was a faint resemblance between the two men. "And a cigar—you don't know how long it's been since I've had a good cigar.

These days there are mostly women looking in on me, and you just can't have a woman buying you one of those.''

Graham laughed. "And a cigar," he promised.

"I'll be looking forward to hearing from you again. 'Bout time we got to know each other," Howard added.

Graham retrieved Lindsey's card and wrote on the back of it. "These are my phone numbers. I want you to feel free to call, even just to talk, but especially if you need anything at all."

"Just a little company's always nice."

"I'll definitely be back," Graham assured him.

The old man saw them to the door.

But just as they were leaving, Graham said, "I'm going to send a couple of things over this afternoon so be expecting your doorbell to ring."

His uncle looked curious, but Graham took Lindsey's arm and escorted her to his car without giving anyone the chance to ask what he had up his sleeve.

Lindsey's curiosity was satisfied once they got into his car and he used the cellular phone to arrange three things for Howard Douglas, at no small expense to have them delivered on such short notice—a new color television, a prime-rib dinner from the best restaurant in town and a box of cigars that cost more than Lindsey spent on groceries for a month.

But from what she was coming to know about this man, none of it surprised her. Nor did she doubt he would keep in touch with his uncle now that he'd reconnected with the old man and make sure he never wanted for anything.

Graham Dunn was a genuinely nice guy. A good person.

And seeing that in action only made him all the more attractive.

Not that he needed to be when his appeal to her was already running out of control.

LORI SPRINGER didn't show up at Graham's house until after nine o'clock that night—more than five hours late. And when she got there she let it be known just what she thought of Graham, of being forced to come and of the ridiculous idea that she was anyone's mother.

Not only did her late arrival come when Kate and Charlie were long past their bedtime, which left them overtired and cranky, but her shouting scared them into wailings that kept pace with Lori Springer's tantrum.

Through it all, the blonde stayed several feet away from them as if they had something contagious, and the twins didn't even respond to Graham's or Lindsey's attempts to comfort them, let alone willingly go near the woman who was shouting her displeasure and frightening them to death.

"Well, so much for my idea," Graham said when Lori had left and the twins were finally put down for the night.

"I wonder," Lindsey mused out loud as they headed down the hall from the guest room.

"What do you wonder?"

"If Lori's antics tonight were planned. If she's ever lived in the same house with the babies, even while someone else takes care of them, she must know nine o'clock is late for them—that they'd be contrary. Then she came in like a wild woman, shrieking and hostile. What kid would have cozied up to that even if she were their mother?"

"Good point," he said. "Let's discuss it over a glass of wine."

"I still have to drive home," she declined, though the sudden arm he put around her shoulders headed her away from the front door and in the direction of the kitchen, anyway.

He poured them both iced tea instead. "So you're giving up on the family-connections theory and coming over to my side in thinking the kids are really mine?"

"I didn't know we were taking sides. But no, I'm not convinced about anything yet. I'm only saying that the way tonight went doesn't necessarily prove the twins belong to Lori Springer or don't belong to Lori Springer."

"How do you think the twins fit into the picture my uncle painted of Charmayne then—when she's long married with a nearly grown daughter, probably living an ordinary life and minding her own business in Colorado Springs?"

Lindsey accepted the glass of tea he held out to her. "The picture he painted was from a long time ago. Any number of things could have happened since then."

"Such as?" he challenged, putting that arm around her again and moving her into the family room, where only one lamp was lit, leaving the darkly paneled space dim and very inviting.

It flashed through Lindsey's mind that suddenly the evening was gaining a datelike feeling and that she shouldn't let it.

But in spite of that she sat on the overstuffed sofa and postulated for him. "Okay, how about what's happening in a gazillion homes right now—divorce, remarriage, a second round of childbearing with husband

number two, which leaves big gaps in the ages of the kids from the new and the kids from the old?''

Graham sat so close beside her that his thigh ran the length of hers. "All right," he conceded. "Your scenario could explain a wide spread in ages, but it doesn't explain why I have Kate and Charlie and a note that says I'm their father."

"A second divorce?" Lindsey went on guessing. "She's already raising one or more kids alone from the first marriage and knows how tough it is, or maybe just plain can't afford the twins, too. So she starts to think about that half brother she's heard of, maybe she saw the same article your uncle and I saw, and 'Hello, Graham, you're a daddy.'"

"I don't believe that," he admitted. "And not just because I'm getting so attached to these babies I can't imagine that I'm not their father—"

Lindsey felt compelled to jump in on that. "Getting attached to two adorable, funny, endearing little kids does not mean you're their father. It can happen between perfect strangers."

"Okay, but still, I may have learned belatedly what kind of person Lori Springer is, but I know now that she's capable of anything, including abandoning her own kids if it suited her purpose. How likely is it that my own half sister is also someone who would do that?"

"You never know. Sometimes people come up with a reason for what they do that you never thought of and it can make a lot of things excusable."

"I'd be surprised to hear anything that excuses this." He frowned into his glass for a moment and then, as if shaking off whatever dark thoughts he'd been in, he stretched an arm across the back of the couch cush-

ions—near enough that Lindsey could feel him even though he wasn't actually touching her. "So I'll bet we're headed for Colorado Springs," he said.

"*I* am," she confirmed.

"You don't think I'm going to let you track down the sister and niece I've never met without being there to meet them, do you?"

"What about the twins?"

"We'll take them along."

"As easy as that? By now you should know doing anything with two babies is complicated. Traveling is the worst."

"It'll be fine," he assured. "I'll get a suite at the Four Seasons with enough bedrooms for all of us and we can stay as long as we need to."

Lindsey's doubts must have been evident in her expression because he went on even before she said anything.

"Besides, we might need Kate and Charlie's reaction to my sister the way we did to Lori Springer. Only this time we won't give advance warning so a stunt like tonight can be staged."

And that seemed to be that.

Not that Lindsey had a good argument against it. At least not one she could use. She wasn't likely to tell him their going away together was a bad idea because she was beginning to realize she just might be a little crazy about him.

Then he said, "I'll make reservations and we can leave tomorrow."

Tomorrow.

Lindsey tensed up at the mere thought of the next day, something she'd been pushing to the back of her mind since that morning, and just like that everything

else took on less importance. "We'll have to go the next day. I need to take some personal time tomorrow."

She hadn't intended for that to sound so ominous but that's how it came out.

"Something special happening?" he asked, and the frown that pulled his brows again told her she'd made him suspicious.

She could have kicked herself for it. Instead she put on a smile and tried to hide what she'd already let show. "No big deal. There's something I have to do, and then I'll be all yours again on Monday."

He wasn't fooled. "Whatever's going on tomorrow must be pretty bad. You look like you're going to go head-to-head with a ghost."

He'd hit closer to home than he knew.

"Want to talk about it?" he asked.

"There isn't anything to talk about. I just have to say goodbye to someone tomorrow and I'm not looking forward to it. Really, it isn't a big deal."

Liar, liar, liar.

He seemed to know it but he only said, "Is there anything I can do?"

This time her smile was genuine as she looked at his handsome face. "You think you can take on the troubles of the world, don't you?"

"Not the whole world, but some of the troubles in my corner of it."

And it felt good to be in his corner of it even if her problems weren't something he could help with. "Thanks, but there's nothing you can do. Nothing anyone can do."

"No dragons I can slay for you?" he joked.

"I was raised with two older brothers, and I never let them fight my battles for me. It's too late for that to

start now. Besides, this isn't a battle. It's just something I have to do that I don't want to."

He nodded, holding her eyes with his incredible blue ones. Somehow his hand had moved from the back of the couch to her nape, where his fingertips smoothed away her stress in a slow, sensuous, feather-light stroke.

"I could kiss it and make it better," he offered, this time only half joking.

"That might work," she heard herself flirt back as if someone else had control over her. "But there isn't one particular spot I could direct you to for that remedy."

"Maybe I could apply it generally," he suggested.

Okay, so she was playing with fire. But at that moment she was enjoying the game too much to deny herself.

Or him, either, when he lowered his mouth to hers in what started as a simple kiss, much like what they'd shared before.

But it didn't stay that way long, as his lips parted and he introduced his tongue to her.

And he clearly didn't mean for the kiss to be only friendly, because he paused just long enough to set both their glasses on the coffee table before taking her fully into his arms and coming back to begin again where he'd left off.

Lindsey gave in to it all. She was tired of fighting herself, her own inclinations, her own feelings and attractions to this man. And before tomorrow she needed the contact of warm human flesh, needed to feel alive and good about herself, as if she were a woman again, a desirable woman....

And no one had ever done that quite as well as Graham had in just the short time she'd known him.

She reached her arms around him, filling her hands with the hardness of his back, and escaped into the paradise of that kiss quieting all the voices in her mind that told her not to.

She met his tongue when it came to toy with hers, matched him circle for circle, thrust for thrust, and then gave way to the sensuous exploration he was intent on doing, reveling in every moment, every sensation, every spark that came to life as things that had been sleeping inside her awoke.

All the while his hands worked magic on her tensed muscles, easing the stress out of her back to leave pure relaxation and languid pleasure in its wake. She melted against him, eager for the feel of that broad, solid chest against breasts left braless in deference to the summer-like heat. Wanting much more than that....

His tongue retreated, inviting hers along, and Lindsey went, discovering the textures of his mouth, the jagged edge of his teeth, how to tease him, torment him, deepen their kiss.

Her hands floated to his hair, to the thick coarseness she'd wondered about, finding something very arousing in that masculine mane.

He deepened their kiss even more, opening his mouth wide, taking hers hungrily, bending her head so far back he had to cradle it in one hand while the other found its way under her shirt to her bare back.

It felt good. As good as she'd imagined it would feel to have that hand against her breast, against her nipple that was hard and straining for his touch.

Her spine arched in response to that thought, that desire, and she couldn't resist sliding her own hands under his shirt in encouragement.

Not that that was the only reason.

Since seeing his bare torso she'd been fantasizing about just that—running her flattened palms along the honed hills and valleys of his back, the defined pectorals of his front.

And as glorious as it had been to feast her eyes on, it was even more glorious to feel. Rippling, rolling muscles. Taut tendons. Sleek, silky skin...

And nipples, kerneled only slightly, but enough to let her know he wasn't immune to what was building between them any more than she was.

One final thrust of his tongue, one final kiss of his lips, and he deserted her mouth, trailing other, smaller kisses along her jaw, down her throat to the hollow, into the small V left by the open top buttons of her shirt.

Then, just when she thought she might explode if he didn't, he slipped a hand around her side to her breast.

Bliss.

His palm was warm and gentle and arousing at once, covering the crest, letting that hardened nib nudge into his palm for a moment before he found it with his fingers and worked a magic that brought every nerve ending in her body to the surface of her skin, yearning, craving more. More of the wonders he could work. More of him.

She wanted them both free of the clothes that were only in the way. She wanted their naked bodies pressed so close together they wouldn't be able to tell where one started and the other left off. She wanted him to take her to that big bed of his at the end of the hall, to make love to her all night long. To wake with him tomorrow morning and do it all again.

Tomorrow.

The sudden memory of what lay in store for her the next day was like a bucket of cold water thrown on her.

"No," she forced herself to say, more a moan than anything.

It was so passion-filled that Graham didn't take it seriously. "No what?" he joked, rolling her nipple between his fingers in a way that weakened her willpower even more.

"I can't do this tonight," she managed in an agony of disappointed desires.

This time his hand slipped away from her breast, and for a moment she had to fight to keep from putting it back, from telling him she hadn't meant it, that she wanted him more than she wanted to breathe.

But instead she sat up straighter, pulling her own hands out from beneath his shirt. "I'm not at a good time in my life," she confessed quietly. "And you're a client—who may be a father."

He smiled down at her. "Who may be a father," he repeated, sounding confused and amused at once.

"This just isn't good."

"I thought it was great."

"You know what I mean."

"Not exactly," he said. "But I suppose I can guess. The situation that's brought us together isn't great and you have a million reasons why we shouldn't get involved."

"At least a million."

"So do I. But none of them make a damn bit of difference when we're together."

She understood that all too well because she experienced the phenomenon herself. "Something has to make a difference," she said. "It's just too soon for me... I'm not ready."

That made him draw completely away from her, leaning against the arm of the sofa.

And as soon as he was gone, she ached to have him back again.

"Then you better go home, Lindsey," he said kindly but with a hint of warning in his voice. "Because tonight I am ready. And if you stay—" he shrugged and shook his head "—I'm going to persuade you that you are, too."

Oh, yes! a part of her shouted. Her whole body was screaming that she really was as ready as he, urging her to fall into his arms again and let what had begun find its natural conclusion.

But she couldn't let herself and she knew it.

So instead she took his warning and stood, heading for the front door.

Graham followed her, and once again she seized business to conceal what was really going on with her. "I'll be at home all day, so if something urgent comes up you can call me there."

"Okay."

Her purse was near the door and she picked it up before turning to face him again, as if it would keep her from throwing herself back into his arms the way she longed to.

"Good night," she said.

He only stared at her, long and hard, his eyes pinning her in place, as if he were trying to find an explanation in her face.

Then he pulled her up tight against him for one more forceful, knee-weakening kiss that very nearly severed the weak thread of her resolve to resist him.

But before that happened he ended the kiss and let her go.

Reaching behind her, he opened the door and held it for her, and Lindsey slipped out to escape the temptation to stay.

He went all the way to her car with her, not saying anything, and opened that door for her, too.

"Good night," she repeated as she got in.

"Yeah, it was," he said with a small smile. "A very good night—at least at the end." Then he closed the car door firmly and bent through the open window to peck one last, chaste kiss on her lips. "Drive safely, Lindsey."

She started the engine and backed out of the drive, with him giving a little push as if it were the only way she could get into motion.

And as she rolled farther away from him, she made herself keep her eyes on her rearview mirror rather than looking at him even one last time tonight.

Because if she did, she knew she just might pull up that driveway again, turn off the engine and follow him inside, after all.

Where she could lose herself in Graham and the wonderful way he made her feel. . . .

And try to make tomorrow never come.

Rober... Calling Charlie for that was the day before.
T... ambiguous reservations for today.

Graham was used to being where the groups — and her
and he wanted to know now, before wondering to...
anxiety.

That idea. What was going on with her today wasn't...
the only thing he wanted to know about her. He wanted
to know everything. Fix wanted all the white milling
about her, about... so far as the tables. New...
about her. And after than some the quake of over...
he wanted to know Lindsey. Stumm... the moment...

...and that was 100% fact...

Chapter Six

By five o'clock the next afternoon Graham was on his
way to Lindsey's house and wondering how wise it was
for him to be doing it.

She'd said she needed a personal day. That she had to
do something she didn't want to do. Say goodbye to
someone she didn't want to say goodbye to.

She'd said there was nothing he could help with. That
she didn't want him slaying dragons for her.

But there he was, on his way to her house just the
same.

Uninvited.

Unannounced.

Maybe unwelcome.

But he'd spent the whole day watching the clock,
wondering if the unpleasantness she faced today was
over yet, wanting to be there for her.

And being eaten alive by curiosity.

Okay, there was nothing noble about being nosy.

But dammit, she kept such a cloak of mystery around
herself, what did she expect? Two car seats when she
didn't have any kids. Familiarity with a pediatrician.
Her reaction to just the mention of someone named

Bobby. Calling Charlie by that name the day before. The ambiguous explanations for today....

Graham wanted to know what was going on with her, and he wanted to know it now, before wondering drove him crazy.

But then, what was going on with her today wasn't the only thing he wanted to know about her. He wanted to know everything. They spent all their time talking about him, about the case, about the babies. Never about her. And more than solving the puzzle of events, he wanted to know Lindsey Strummel, the woman.

The woman he was so attracted to, it was nearly reaching a fever pitch.

And that was another reason he was going to her house—because that fever pitch made it so he couldn't stand going a day without seeing her.

"Oh, you've got it bad," he told himself as he weaved in and out of highway traffic in his hurry to get to her.

But he couldn't deny it.

She'd been on his mind almost constantly since he'd first set eyes on her. Even in the midst of this current mess in his life.

And despite that mess, he'd enjoyed every minute they were together, he couldn't wait to see her every day, he hated to see her leave at night. And in between? He just couldn't get enough of her.

But then, they were so good together.

Good at bouncing ideas and theories back and forth. Good with the twins. Good at teasing each other out of tense times. Good at kissing....

His feelings were a long way from anything even resembling what should be between a client and his investigator, and they were sending him to her doorstep even when she probably didn't want him there.

But he couldn't help himself. Not even reminders of the pitfalls—which could well be down the road if he let himself get involved with a woman who wasn't free of her past—could calm what was growing inside him.

And today, though he didn't understand how, he knew she needed someone with her, no matter what she'd said. And he wanted to be that someone.

Who was he kidding?

He wanted to be the only one.

LINDSEY THOUGHT she was emotionally prepared for what she had to face, but when her doorbell rang her heart leaped into her throat, her stomach cramped into a hard knot and she could barely breathe.

Maybe it hadn't been such a good idea to tell Logan and Quinn to stay away.

Her feet seemed glued to the tweed carpet of her small mauve-colored bedroom. All of a sudden she felt very cold, and her head was so light she had to grab on to the oak chest of drawers to steady herself.

Maybe she shouldn't let them in. Maybe she should just hide out in the bedroom. Under the bed. With her hands over her ears.

Or maybe she should open the front door, grab Bobby and shut Dave out.

Oh, good, now she'd lost her mind.

She could just see the headlines—P.I. Goes Berserk and Holds Former Stepson Hostage.

Not a pretty picture.

And too ridiculous to be anything more than a fleeting bit of insanity that she would never do.

But then, she wasn't doing anything. She was just standing there when the doorbell rang again.

"Move, legs," she said, forcing a full breath into her lungs, exhaling it slowly and trying to ease her shoulders down into their normal position. "One step, two steps, three steps . . ." She counted them off as she took them, sounding as enthusiastic as a dueler with double vision, until she made it to the front door.

Another steeling breath and she even managed to open it.

But standing on her front porch was not her former husband and stepson.

It was Graham, looking so wonderful in a pair of khaki slacks and a pale blue sport shirt that she could have jumped into his arms.

Or maybe she was just so glad not to be alone after all, that anyone would have looked wonderful.

Except that he really did. And just his being there suddenly made her feel better.

"Look," he began without a greeting, "I know you said there was nothing I could do for you but I've been having Lindsey withdrawal over not getting to see you today, so I figured whatever was going on was probably over by now and maybe you'd let me take you to dinner or just hold your hand or—"

"It isn't over. In fact, when the doorbell rang I thought it was my ex-husband. He's due here any minute."

The grimace on Graham's face was so exaggerated it was comical, and although Lindsey wouldn't have believed it possible, it actually made her laugh, albeit a little hysterically.

"That's who you're saying goodbye to? Your ex-husband? God. No wonder you didn't want me around. I'll get out of here." He began to go, but on its own her hand shot out to his arm to stop him.

"I'm not saying goodbye to my ex-husband. Every-thing between us is past. I'm saying goodbye to his son, Bobby. He was my stepson." She was barely making sense and she knew it. But at that moment it was the best she could do. "Even though I thought I was up to facing this on my own, I've never been as glad to see anyone in my life as I am to see you right now."

That seemed to please him, and the slow-spreading smile on that wonderful face of his warmed her clammy skin.

"Come in, please," she invited, fighting the urge to yank on his arm. Instead she let go of it and moved back a step so he could join her in the entryway that was only separated from her living room by a bookcase.

"Will my being here cause problems?"

"The problems are all over with. Unless maybe you'd rather not be here."

He slipped an arm around the small of her back, pulled her up to him and stopped her words with an old-movie kiss.

Oddly enough, that impromptu kiss and the support it gave helped to ground her, to put to rest the last rem-nants of the panic that had struck when the doorbell rang the first time.

And even when it sounded again just then, it only made her pulse speed up slightly, rather than raising that same level of anxiety.

Graham let her go, glanced at the door, then back at her. "Shall I stay here or would you rather I wait out of sight?"

"Here is fine," she said, her voice much more quiet than she'd meant for it to be.

But still, the prospect of reopening the door to her ex-husband didn't loom as large as it had moments before.

And this time when she answered the bell her ex-husband was exactly who was there.

Along with Bobby.

Lindsey barely spared the tall, dark-haired man she'd been married to a glance and a hello before dropping her gaze to the little boy at his side, a miniature version in appearance, with black hair that waved all over his head and big round ebony eyes.

"Lindsey!" he shouted over his father's greeting. "It's still me! You didn't forget me, did you?"

Lindsey squatted down on her heels and held her arms wide. "Forget you? How could I ever, ever do that?"

The small child moved into her embrace, clamping himself to her neck in a tight hug.

And Lindsey hugged him back. Hard. Close. Just as tight. Thinking once more of pushing her former husband out the door and keeping his son.

Then Bobby released his hold on her to dig into the pocket of his corduroy pants, which were riding so low the rolled cuffs draped the front of his tennis shoes and dusted the floor in back.

"I brought you something."

"Why don't we go inside?" she suggested as he searched. Then she noticed the two men sizing each other up—Dave from the tiled entranceway and Graham from just behind her—and remembered her manners.

"Dave, this is my…" What? Client? No, Graham was much more than that, and at that moment she admitted it to herself. She settled on, "…my friend, Gra-

ham Dunn," although that, too, seemed inadequate. "Graham, this is Dave Morrisy. And this is Bobby," she finished, ruffling up the little boy's hair. "He'll be four next month."

Graham offered his hand to Dave and they shook warily, each clearly suspicious of the other. But at that moment Lindsey didn't care if they danced together or drew daggers. Bobby was all she was interested in.

He finally found what he was looking for. He held it out to Lindsey as she urged everyone into the living room. "It's one of the seashells we got at Disneyland before."

The mention of that trip they'd all enjoyed a year earlier stabbed Lindsey like a knife. She smiled to hide it and took the shell. "Are you sure you don't want to keep it? I know you like to have them all on your dresser to look at."

"Now you can look at that one, like me."

Lindsey closed her hand around it and held it to her heart. "Thank you."

"Now say your goodbyes, Bobby, we have to get going," her ex-husband instructed.

"We just got here," Bobby told him with a frown.

"I told you we could only stay a minute."

The joy seemed to go out of Bobby with that. He turned his frown on Lindsey. "I don't like that you're not my mama no more. And I told that doctor man about it, and he said my dad should let me say goodbye before we go to Kentucky, but I don't want to say goodbye. I want you to come with us and be my mama again like you was."

Lindsey's fist clenched so tight around the shell that it bit into her palm. But she didn't let up. That pain

helped distract her from the much, much bigger one tearing through her at that moment.

"Bobby," Dave said in a warning tone.

His son and Lindsey both ignored him. Lindsey knelt down in the middle of the living room floor so she could be at eye level with the child and pulled him nearer with both hands on his narrow hips. "You know I can't go with you, honey," she said in a voice that didn't betray any of what was going on inside her.

"Don't you want to?" he accused.

"It isn't that."

"It's my dad, huh? Him and you don't like each other no more."

"Let's not go through this again, Bobby," Dave warned again. "We've talked about it and you know Lindsey can't come with us. We just came here today to say goodbye, and we have to get to the airport."

Bobby lunged into a second grip of Lindsey's neck, though this time it wasn't just a boisterous hug. He was hanging on for dear life. "I don't like this divorce."

"I know, baby. I know," Lindsey muttered soothingly, at a complete loss for what else to say. Shoving Dave out the door to kidnap his son was seeming less and less crazy by the minute.

He pried Bobby away, and the child didn't put up much of a struggle, accepting the inevitable now that he'd at least tried to change it. He leaned against his father's leg.

"Bye, Lindsey," he said as if this were the part he'd rehearsed.

"You be a good boy for your dad," she answered, but only in a bare whisper around the lump in her throat.

"When I'm all grown up I'll come back and get you to marry me," he promised.

That made her smile even as a tear sneaked down her cheek in spite of how hard she was fighting not to cry.

"I'll be here," she told him.

Dave swung the little boy up into his arms, drawing Lindsey's gaze. "Take care, Lindsey," he said.

"Yeah. You, too." She couldn't trust herself to get close enough to kiss Bobby so she kissed her fingertips and held them out to him as if it would get to him that way.

Then her ex-husband took his son and left. And she tortured herself by watching at the window until they were in the car and gone completely.

But strangely enough, that single tear that had slipped out before wasn't joined by the torrent she'd expected. And though she felt as if her heart had been wrenched out by the roots, there was also a certain sense of relief that what she'd been dreading—her last moment with the child who had been like her own since he was a baby, the child she'd had to accept the loss of months ago—was over.

"Lindsey? Are you okay?"

The sound of Graham's deep voice washed over her like balm. When she turned from the window she found him very close behind her. Close enough that he had only to raise his arms to wrap them around her.

And before she'd even thought about it, she was enveloped in the strength of his big body, her cheek against his chest, her own arms encircling his waist.

He pressed his lips to her head and stayed there, letting the warmth of his breath heat her scalp, completing the sense she had of being cocooned by him.

She closed her eyes and listened to the steady beat of his heart, let herself drift away on it as her pores drank in the solace of being held.

It was only when that solace began to turn to something more, something on the verge of sensuous, that she knew she'd weathered the storm. With Graham's help.

She eased away from him a bit and smiled up at him. "Thanks."

"For what? I didn't do anything," he said. And then, grinning with only one side of his mouth, he added, "Yet."

So he'd felt the subtle alteration in what they were sharing, too. Still, she could only deal with so much at once and right now anything romantic was beyond her limits.

She took a step backward. "Where are the twins?" she asked in an attempt to get things back to normal.

His smile was patient, as if he knew what she was doing and would go along with it. "I called Annie to stay with them awhile."

"And she came, even on a Sunday?"

"I told you she's a gem. Besides, she likes you, and when I said I thought you had some trouble today and I wanted to be with you, she was glad to help out." He crossed his arms over his chest, shifted his weight more to one hip than the other and seemed to be surveying her. "So how about it? Will you let me take you to dinner and hold your hand?"

"Before it was an either-or offer. Now you want to do both?"

"Absolutely."

Lindsey hesitated. She was still ragged around the edges despite her efforts to conceal it, and it didn't seem

fair to inflict that on him. "I don't think I'm good company tonight," she confessed.

"You can sit and stare into space if you want. I only have one question and then if you don't say another word all evening I'll understand."

She arched her eyebrows and raised her chin, waiting for it.

"Two car seats—why, if there was only Bobby?"

"When he was a baby we had two cars so we had two car seats—one for each. Then he outgrew them and they were left in the garage until you inherited them."

"Whew! I was imagining much worse."

"You hid it well."

"As well as I'm hiding all the rest of my curiosity about what's going on with you."

He now deserved to have that curiosity satisfied, she decided. And after spending all day pacing her house in nervous anticipation of seeing Bobby, she discovered that the prospect of getting it all out was suddenly appealing. "Let me get myself together and I'll fill you in over dinner," she finally said, accepting his invitation.

"And the hand-holding?"

She only smiled.

"Whenever you're ready," he answered, making it clear she could take her own good time dressing, choosing when to explain to him, and when to hold his hand, too.

And she did take her own good time. First as she changed into a pair of black stirrup pants and a silk blouse. Then as she combed her hair and applied a little blush to soften the harsh pallor of her skin. And finally by spending the drive to Ristorante Italia in silence.

But once they were seated in the quiet restaurant, which occupied a replica of an old train station on the perimeter of the Heritage Square shops and amusement park in the foothills of Golden, it seemed like a good place to open up to him.

"I used to be a social worker," she began after they'd ordered.

"So that's your connection to social services. You mentioned you had one when you took the twins and me on, and I wondered. And the other connection you said you had—the police—that would be your brother?"

"Right. For a little while longer at least, but that's another story. Anyway, Dave Morrisy started out as a case I was assigned. His wife had died in childbirth and her parents had accused him of being an unfit father."

"I take it he wasn't?"

"No. He was inexperienced at caring for a child, but the truth of the matter was that the in-laws didn't like him and wanted custody of Bobby, so accusing him of abuse was the route they took in an attempt to get the baby."

"You didn't let that happen."

"Actually, I turned the case over to another person who did the lion's share of the investigation and made the decision."

"Why did you do that?"

"There was an attraction between Dave and I. A strong one. His wife had been dead about three months by the time we met. He was still grieving, but he said he'd also come to grips with needing to go on with his own life. He can be very charming, and when I realized I was susceptible to that, I couldn't risk being swayed by

it. So I bowed out. He passed muster all on his own—without charming the other social worker.''

''So you knew his attraction to you was genuine and not just a snow job?''

''Yes. And once the charges were resolved, I accepted a date with him.''

''And gave in to the attraction.''

''That and a whirlwind courtship. I married him three months later.''

''That would have made Bobby six months old?''

Their salads arrived to interrupt them. But when the waitress left, Lindsey knew she couldn't avoid what he was thinking. Much as she'd like to.

''Six months old, yes. Just how long Dave had been widowed. And you don't have to say it. I know I must have been out of my mind to marry him so soon after the death of his wife.''

But that didn't seem to be what Graham would have said even had she given him the chance, because when he answered her, there was no judgment in his words or his tone of voice. ''It must not have seemed like the wrong thing to do or you wouldn't have done it.''

''No, it didn't. Although my family wanted me to hold off and friends warned me it was too soon. But I didn't listen to anyone. Sure, he'd just lost his wife and he had a baby who needed a mother, but frankly, it was insulting to have people who were close to me thinking all he saw in me was an instant replacement. I loved him. I believed he loved me.''

''Except your family and friends were right and you really were just a quick fix for his problems?'' he asked sympathetically.

"Basically. But Dave doesn't get all the blame. The rescuer in me was at work, too, and I just wasn't recognizing it. Plus there was one other big, big factor."

"Bobby."

She nodded. "I'd fallen as much in love with him as I had with Dave. Maybe even more."

Memories of the child she'd honestly believed she would raise to adulthood assaulted her just then and she had to fight them off. It took until Graham's lasagna and her eggplant in marinara sauce arrived before she thought she could go on.

"It wasn't as if Dave didn't love me at all or I didn't love him," she explained. "But the trouble was that loving each other was only a portion of the reason we got together. And maybe not the biggest portion."

She paused to taste her food and then continued. "It took me a long time to face it, but needing a mother for his son was definitely one of Dave's motives for marriage. Not that I'm sure it was conscious—I don't believe he married me rather than hiring a diaper service. But certainly he wanted to provide Bobby with a mom. And my feelings for Bobby were a huge factor in deciding to marry Dave. I wanted to be that mom," she admitted.

"But both of you loving his son wasn't enough to keep the marriage going?"

"For me it might have been. But for Dave..." She shook her head sadly. "Rebound relationships. Transitional relationships. The pop-psychology terms applied. Marrying me got him through a rough patch in his life. It cushioned his grief, it gave him time to become comfortable with being a father, learn the ropes. But once that rough patch smoothed out, I guess he

looked up and found that I wasn't the woman he really wanted to spend the rest of his life with.''

"Bet he'd found someone who was," Graham said with so much disgust it was almost palpable in the air.

Again Lindsey nodded. "On a trip he and Bobby took without me, to visit his family in Kentucky. He met up with his high school sweetheart.''

"I'm sorry.''

"It was a blow to my ego, I won't deny it.''

"And when he exited the marriage, he took Bobby with him.''

Even in the midst of recounting the worst thing that had ever happened to her, she couldn't help smiling at him. "Were you there? You only seem to need me to flesh out the details.''

"I'm just fitting it all together with what I've been imagining since meeting you. I'm equipped with several possible scenarios.''

"I'd have thought you had more things to think about than me.''

"You'd be surprised how hard it is for me to think about anything but you.''

That pleased her much more than it should have. She tamped down on it and went back to talking about Bobby. "Technically, I was only the stepmother. I didn't have any rights to a child who wasn't mine either biologically or legally. And it didn't matter that I loved him as if he were my own, that I'd raised him from the time he was a small baby. Dave wanted out of the marriage. He didn't want anything to do with me—out of guilt, I suppose—and that meant I was completely cut off from Bobby.''

"Wasn't there something you could do?''

"Nothing. I even went to court asking for visitation privileges. But it didn't matter. Dave's plans to move back to Kentucky were in place. He told the judge that he wouldn't be returning to Denver for any reason and that he wanted my ties with Bobby severed as cleanly as possible, that encouraging the attachment between the two of us would only hurt his son when it came time to leave, and that once they had I wouldn't ever see him again, anyway."

"And the judge honored his wishes."

She nodded yet again. "He ruled in favor of Dave. We separated eight months ago, and until today I hadn't seen Bobby for the last six of them."

"Then how did today come about?"

"I understand that Bobby wouldn't give up the idea of seeing me before they left Denver and the therapist Dave has been consulting sided with Bobby. Or I'd have never seen him again at all."

"Did you want to do this today?" Graham asked gently, his penetrating blue eyes watching her intently.

"I had mixed emotions. When the divorce was final three months ago I asked Dave to let me say goodbye to Bobby, but he wouldn't agree to it. After that I really had to come to grips with losing him, so I wasn't anxious to open that wound again. But I also couldn't deny Bobby—or myself—the one last time together that Dave was finally willing to allow." She analyzed her own feelings for a moment as some things sunk in for the first time.

"Actually," she mused out loud, "I feel as if this really closed this part of my life for me. I've spent a lot of time and energy dealing with all my emotions—licking my wounds, I guess you could say—and I'm in better shape than I realized before. Saying goodbye today re-

ally seems to have helped put it behind me." And it felt good.

"So what happened to you with Bobby is why you keep warning me not to get attached to Charlie and Kate, isn't it?" Graham said after a moment.

"The voice of experience."

"And why you do that little dance around them."

"What dance is that?"

"You try to avoid them, but one look at them and you're drawn like a moth to a flame. This case must be rough on you."

"Parts of it," she admitted.

"But not all of it?" he fished, holding her eyes with the glint in his.

"No, not all of it. In fact, not most of it. I'm enjoying being at work again."

His smile was slow, as if he knew she'd just skirted telling him that *he* was what she was enjoying.

"So you're on your feet again? Recovered and running at full speed?"

"Yes, I am," she answered confidently because she suddenly knew it was true.

The check came while they were talking, and since they'd both finished eating, Graham paid the bill and they left. But rather than taking her straight home, he stopped at the park where they'd gone picnicking with the twins so they could walk around the lake.

That was when he held her hand.

But hand-holding was all he did as he made her laugh with tales of the early days of Dunnit Tennis Shoes, of starting his business on a shoestring—"no pun intended," he assured her. Of shipments of soleless shoes, and of the factory mistake that had produced some of his bestsellers in fuchsia and thereby proved that exotic

colors were not only marketable but could be very popular.

And if anyone had told Lindsey that this day would have ended as pleasantly as it did she would never have believed it. But pleasantly was just how it ended.

By the time Graham took her home she actually felt great. Freer. Happier. Stronger than she had in months.

"Thanks," she repeated as they headed up to her house.

"Why does that sound like more than simple appreciation for a nice dinner?" he asked, smiling down at her in the glow of the porch light.

"Because it is for more than a nice dinner, although dinner was very nice."

"What else is it for?"

She shrugged. "I guess for just being here today in case I had fallen on my face," she joked.

"For that you're welcome."

He tipped her chin up with his fingertips and kissed her. Softly. Chastely. And somehow she sensed that he knew she'd been on enough of an emotional roller coaster today without taking a ride through passion now. So although his kiss was warm and wonderful and sent sweet honey on a slow roll all through her, he didn't deepen it.

And while she longed for more, she also knew this was best. For tonight, anyway.

When he ended the kiss, he said, "Don't forget to pack your bags. Our reservations at The Four Seasons in Colorado Springs are all set for tomorrow."

Something about the way he said that excluded the fact that they'd have the twins along and seemed to promise things a business trip shouldn't.

Or maybe it was just her own mind filling in the possibilities of being with him in a hotel suite. But either way, excited shivers ran up her spine.

And for once she didn't chastise herself for it.

And she didn't fight it, either.

"I'd like to get an early start," she said.

"Want to bring your things and stay the night at my place? I have a third bedroom, you know. Then we can leave at dawn. I guarantee Kate and Charlie as reliable alarm clocks."

The words made that seem innocent enough, but this time there was no doubt that his tone and the single, sexy raised eyebrow that went with it made it sound like an invitation to much more.

And though it was tempting, Lindsey declined the offer. "I don't think we need to start out *that* early."

He grinned as if he'd known he was going to be turned down but had had to give it the old college try, anyway. "You're the boss," he said, taking her by the shoulders to kiss her once more, quickly, before he let her go completely. "I'll see you in the morning, then."

"Mmm. 'Night," she murmured as he turned and headed back to his car.

And as she watched him leave, for a change she didn't fight the delicious tingling sensation his kiss had left behind, or the pleasure of looking at his terrific derriere in those well-cut slacks, or even the fantasies of what might be yet to come.

Because at that moment it all felt too good.

And for the first time she thought that maybe she'd earned the right to indulge just a little in those good feelings.

And in Graham and this time they had together.

Chapter Seven

All things considered, the drive to Colorado Springs with the twins the next morning went pretty well. After two diaper changes and a snack stop, they made it to The Four Seasons hotel shortly before noon.

The plan was for Graham to check them in, get the babies some lunch and put them down for a nap while Lindsey went to work. Then, if she located Graham's half sister in the course of that work, she'd arrange for him to meet the woman.

The hotel suite he'd reserved for them was complete with three bedrooms, a kitchen and a living room, and as Graham dealt with Kate, Charlie, two bellmen and the bags, Lindsey checked the local phone book.

"Bingo," she murmured to herself when she found Charmayne's husband listed. It wasn't often that she got that lucky twice on the same case, but why question good fortune?

She wrote down the address and phone number, as well as the phone and room numbers for the hotel. Then she found Graham changing Charlie's diaper on the bed in his room.

Or at least trying to change Charlie's diaper.

Although Graham was now adept at the chore, after the long car ride both kids were antsy and he was having trouble getting Charlie to lie still. Graham would barely get one or two snaps of the baby's overalls fastened before Charlie would try to crawl off and Graham would have to pull him back.

And while this was going on, Kate was into everything—flinging bibs and toys out of the diaper bag, trying to bite through a tube of ointment and squishing it out from a hole that popped open in the bottom. Tasting the ointment and then spitting it out. And finally managing to open the lid on the baby powder, squeezing it to send a geyser of the white stuff to clot into the ointment and cling to the baby wipes Charlie had latched on to and was pulling out as fast as his little fists could grasp them.

"Looks like this is a good time for me to get out of here," Lindsey said with a laugh as she hurried to the bedside to rescue the powder from Kate before the mess got any worse.

"Oh, sure, when the going gets tough—"

"The smart leave," she finished over Kate's informing her she was hungry.

"Coward," Graham accused.

"Through and through." But she didn't go anywhere. Instead she snatched the ointment tube from Kate just as the little girl was about to try a second taste.

"What's first on your agenda?" Graham asked as he wrestled the baby wipe from Charlie.

"I hate to admit it, but I found Norris Planter's name in the phone book. I'll start there."

"Maybe I ought to go and you ought to stay here," he suggested, his frustration sounding.

"No way!" She took the carton of wipes away from Charlie and handed him a toy key ring to replace it.

It didn't appease him, but at least for the moment before he threw it, Graham managed to finish diapering him. This time when he rolled to make a getaway, Graham let him.

"Think you'll be gone long?" he asked as they both gathered powdery, ointmenty, wasted baby wipes and threw them away.

"I don't know. I'll call and keep you posted if I don't end up back here in an hour with the case solved."

"A couple of lucky breaks in the phone book and the woman is cocky," he teased as they finished cleaning up.

"Hey, this is pure talent and skill," she countered.

"Yeah, right."

In a motion as quick as lightning he stopped what he was doing and pulled her to him, locking his arms around her waist. Then he gave her a devilish wiggle of his eyebrows and said, "One of these days I'm going to show you my talent and skill."

She played dumb. "In tennis shoes?"

"Out of them."

Be still my heart, she thought. But she only laughed and said, "Why do I get the feeling that the line between client and investigator has been crossed?"

"Is that the only feeling you have?"

"No, I also have the feeling I'd better get out of here right now or I might not get out at all." Not that she'd mind if she didn't. She was enjoying this silly banter and being in his arms in a way that seemed so comfortable, such a perfect fit, that it was as if they'd been ending up there for years and years.

Something had changed between them today and she couldn't really put her finger on it. She was more relaxed now that saying goodbye to Bobby was past, and that might be part of it. But it really was as if they'd crossed some imaginary line and left behind any pretense that what was going on between them was a professional relationship.

Several times during the drive from Denver, Graham had reached over the gearshift and squeezed her hand or her arm or her shoulder. And she'd not only let him, she'd welcomed it. She'd squeezed his hand back. She'd even found herself angled toward him, reveling in the sight of him, the sound of him, the smell of his aftershave, the very nearness of him.

And something else was different, too.

The voice in her head that cautioned her not to do this wasn't as loud. Or as powerful.

And she wasn't paying much attention even to the whisper of it.

"We could always put off the investigation until tomorrow and spend today just having a good time," Graham said, interrupting her wandering thoughts. "We could take the kids to the zoo."

Tempting. Very tempting. A whole afternoon of just being with him, with the twins. Of joking and laughing. Of being carefree and frivolous. Of holding hands and brushing shoulders and . . .

And even though the voice of caution was faint, it still reminded her she needed not to lose all sight of the fact that she was still supposed to be doing a job for him.

"Sorry. When I have a hot lead, I have to follow up on it," she said like a classic B-movie detective.

He rolled his eyes but let her go, muttering, "A hot lead out of the phone book."

Lindsey caught a glimpse of the twins behind him taste-testing the cotton they'd shredded from a clean diaper lining. She nodded in their direction. "Better get those kids fed or you'll have big problems," she advised. "And I better go to work."

"Hurry back," he ordered, scooping up Kate to pull wet cotton out of her mouth.

"I will," Lindsey answered glibly, almost as if she didn't mean it.

But she did. She would definitely hurry back.

Because even if she couldn't give the whole day over to him, she could give him her whole evening.

UNLIKE LOCATING Graham's uncle, finding his half sister and her family was not quick and easy.

Not that the address was difficult to track down, but once Lindsey got there what she found was a dilapidated house in the middle of a suburban neighborhood, with a four-week-old notice of eviction in the window and no signs of life.

That was when the real work began.

Knocking on doors, asking questions, garnering any piece of information she might be able to follow up on.

And once that tack was exhausted, following up was just what she did.

Her next stop was the library to look through newspaper articles. Then she went to the city records department, and finally to the police station, accumulating copies of everything she could get her hands on along the way.

And though she'd been joking about solving the case in one afternoon, by the time she called it a day, that was basically what she'd done.

IT WAS AFTER SEVEN when Lindsey arrived back at the hotel. Graham and the twins weren't in the room, but there was a note on her pillow saying they'd gone downstairs for a swim.

She hadn't brought a bathing suit, and so rather than hurrying to join them, she took a shower to cool off and wash away the grime and stickiness of having worked away the day out in Colorado's mid-September heat wave.

Then she dressed in a pair of white tennis shorts and a red tank top, dried and combed her hair and applied just a touch of makeup and a few drops of perfume behind her ears. Not because she was spending the evening with Graham, she told herself, but only because she wanted to feel clean and refreshed.

He and the kids still weren't back by then, so she put the room key in her pocket and went to look for them.

The outdoor pool had several noisy, splashing teenagers in it but no sign of Graham, Kate or Charlie, so Lindsey tried the indoor pool. That was where they were, with the smaller version all to themselves.

She didn't go into the glass-enclosed area right away, though. Instead she stood just outside, watching them.

Graham was in the shallow end of the pool with a baby on each hip. The water barely came to his waist, so he had complete control over just how much the twins were submerged.

And that seemed to be the game.

With every step he took he dropped slightly farther into the water until it brushed the kids' chins. Then,

with a great whoosh, he swooped up out of the drink, making them shriek so loudly Lindsey could hear it through the wall of windows.

Graham's handsome face showed how much he was enjoying himself, and Lindsey absorbed the sight.

Sharply sculpted planes and jawbone. That slightly long nose. The lines that etched his eyes and the corners of his supple mouth when he smiled. Straight white teeth that flashed as he laughed....

Down, down, down into the water he went again as if he were descending stairs one at a time, curving his Paul Bunyan shoulders around the twins to say something to them that no doubt built their anticipation of what was to come. And then he rose once more from the water like the mighty sea king rescuing two tiny mortals.

Lindsey's gaze took in that broad, well-honed chest and flat, hard stomach. The power of each of his arms holding the babies against his sides; the smooth, plump little bodies pressed to his rougher, masculine skin, dwarfed by his big body.

And she wanted to be there, too, held to him, touched by him, her own bare flesh against his.

He spun around then to go in the other direction and she memorized the view of his back, too—all the rolling muscles and flexed tendons, the perfect V-shaped sculpture of magnificent man.

Magnificent man delighting in two babies he thought were his.

She finally pushed through the door and went onto the tiled deck that surrounded the small pool, catching Graham's eye as he turned to come her way once more.

And the slow, lazy grin of pleasure he bathed her in drew her all the way to the water's edge.

"Madame Detective," he greeted, doing his own imitation of an old movie by lacing it with mock suspicion. "We were wondering if you'd ever get back to us." Then he lowered one thick eyebrow at her in a comical frown to complete the picture.

"Legwork takes time," she answered glibly.

His gaze dropped to those very appendages and he groaned his appreciation as if it were almost more than he could bear. "And what great gams they are, shweetheart."

"Thanks," she said through a laugh at his switch to a pretty fair Bogart impression. "But this shweetheart needs food. Did you guys eat without me?"

"These two did," he said as if he couldn't believe the babies' audacity. "But I waited for you."

He waded to the steps in the corner of the pool, gave the kids one final dunking to their chins and climbed out.

When Kate and Charlie realized their swim was over they both put up a fuss.

"More!" Kate demanded, while Charlie just tried to escape Graham's arms to get back into the water.

"No more," Graham told them firmly, keeping hold of the slippery Charlie with some difficulty.

They both started to wail, making Graham flinch. "Here, have a kid," he said, dipping to hand Kate to Lindsey.

She picked up a towel first, then accepted the baby while Graham wrapped Charlie in a second one, sat him on a chair so he could slip into a terry-cloth bathrobe himself and then picked him up again.

Over the noise he said, "How about we take them upstairs, rinse the chlorine off of them and get them to

bed? Then, while I shower, you can order room service for us. Can you wait that long to eat?''

''Better that than trying to do it while they cry,'' she agreed and led the way out to the lobby elevators in hopes that once the pool was out of sight the kids might quiet down.

But they were tired and fussy by then and kept at it all the way through the fastest bath in history and getting diapered and dressed in their pajamas.

Luckily, though, when Lindsey and Graham put them in the portable cribs the hotel had in the third bedroom, they both curled up with their respective blanket and monkey and were asleep nearly before the light was out.

''Ah, quiet never sounded so good,'' Graham said on an audible sigh as they pulled the door closed.

''I don't know. Food sounds pretty good to me at this point.''

''Then we'd better get you some. While I have a quick shower why don't you order yourself some dinner and me a rare steak, salad, potato—the works. And don't forget a bottle of wine. No one's driving home tonight,'' he added with a suggestive glint that only partly seemed to be a joke.

Then he pecked a quick, unexpected kiss on her cheek and said, ''I won't be a minute,'' and slipped into his own bedroom.

Okay, so she had an instant flash of following him.

She didn't do it.

Instead she ordered their meals and set her notes and the copies she'd made throughout the afternoon on the coffee table.

It was a sobering enough assortment of information to chase away those untoward thoughts that had wandered into the bedroom with Graham.

He came out about twenty minutes later, dressed in jeans and a white polo shirt, his hair freshly washed and combed, his face clean shaven and smelling of cologne.

His feet were bare, and though she knew it was crazy Lindsey couldn't help being very aware of it, as well as having the sense that it made things seem as intimate as if he were half-naked.

And for just a moment she considered stashing the notes and copies under the sofa cushions so they could concentrate on something else.

But of course that, too, was a fleeting and inappropriate thought that she quelled shortly after it assaulted her.

Though not before she'd slipped off her own shoes.

"What's all this?" he asked with a nod at the papers on the coffee table, noticing them just as there was a knock on the door.

"It's what I found out today," she answered, trying not to watch his rear end as he went to let room service in.

While the waiter arranged everything on a small table out on the balcony that ran the length of the suite, Graham went to the coffee table and glanced down at the array.

He didn't pick up any of what was there, though. He just stared down at it. "Apparently you had a productive day."

"Mmm," she confirmed noncommittally, honestly unsure how he was going to take what she had to tell him.

The waiter went to Graham to have him sign the bill and then left discreetly. But even the soft sound of the door closing behind the man seemed to spur Graham to walk away from the coffee table as if he didn't want to know what information was contained in the papers there.

Instead, with an arm at her waist, he ushered Lindsey onto the balcony.

The wide deck-size platform was dimly lit by candles and the soft glow of light coming from the three sets of French doors that opened onto it from the living room, Graham's bedroom and Lindsey's.

A wine bucket stood beside the white wrought-iron garden table—the bottle she'd ordered already open—and silver-domed plates and crystal goblets waited at each place setting.

Graham held one of the chairs for her, then took the other for himself.

But just when she was beginning to wonder if he really was going to ignore the fact that she'd dug up a lot of information for him today, he poured them both a glass of wine and said, "The twins aren't mine, are they?"

Lindsey didn't see any reason to beat around the bush, but she did keep her voice quiet and consoling. "No, they aren't."

He nodded very slowly, a little sadly, and stayed staring at his own hand around the stem of his glass for a few moments.

Then he reached across the table and lifted the lid on her club sandwich. "I thought you were starved?"

Lindsey was less interested in food than in him. "I know you believed they were your kids."

He smiled at her. "I did," he agreed. "But it hasn't been long enough for me to really get used to the idea, and you didn't let me forget that they might not be, so this isn't on the same level as your losing Bobby."

He knew what she was thinking.

But before she could say anything, he added, "Plus, who can tell, I may end up with them, anyway. Or did you run across someone who wants them back?"

"No, I didn't," she was quick to assure him.

He uncovered his own meal then and cut into his steak. "What did you find?" he asked, seeming recovered from the disappointment and ready to go on.

"Nothing very pretty."

"In this situation I didn't expect you to. Go ahead, give me the cold, hard facts."

Lindsey tasted her sandwich and her wine, and then did just that. "Kate and Charlie are your illegitimate half great-niece and -nephew."

"You *were* busy today. Run it by me in a way I can understand."

"They were born to Charmayne's daughter Francine, who was barely sixteen at the time and apparently had no idea who the father was."

He flinched, swallowed a bite of potato and said, "Then you found Charmayne."

"Not the way you're thinking. She and Francine were killed in a car accident this past February."

"Oh, boy," he breathed in a sorry sigh.

"What I found today at the address in the phone book was a house that had been repossessed. From all reports, Charmayne kept things together in the family. Norris Planter—Charmayne's husband—hadn't been able to keep a job in years due to an alcohol problem. Charmayne was the only source of support for herself,

Planter, Francine and the twins—who she hadn't wanted Francine to give up."

"And when she and Francine were killed, that left Kate and Charlie with Planter."

"Right. And Planter with no income. The neighbors raised the money for the burials—there wasn't any insurance—and even pitched in to help Planter with the babies, hoping he'd get on his feet and take over before too long. But he didn't make any effort to clean up his act or care for the kids or get a job, and the neighbors finally realized he never would. Last month, when he was about to be evicted, someone finally reported the situation to social services. He got wind of it even before they showed up, seemed afraid he was in for charges of abuse or neglect, took the babies and disappeared. One neighbor remembered him saying something about family in Denver, so everyone assumed that was where he'd gone."

"And I was the family in Denver," Graham guessed.

"You or Howard Douglas."

"Howard didn't know anything—"

"People don't always tell the truth, Graham."

"Still."

"I know. It seems unlikely that anyone would leave the twins with that frail old man, or that Howard could have gotten them to your place or persuaded someone else to do it. But he admitted knowing about you from the magazine article and no one I spoke to today mentioned that Planter did."

"That doesn't mean he didn't."

"Granted. Or maybe he showed up at Howard's, Howard told him about it and he took things from there."

"And it doesn't really matter because the bottom line is that *someone* got the twins to me and I'm the only person they have who's either capable of raising them or willing to."

Lindsey had eaten all she wanted of her meal by then and pushed away her plate. "Are you willing to?"

"You mean because they're only distantly related to me rather than being my own kids?"

"And because you're a single man who, as far as I can tell, didn't have any thought of becoming a father a week ago."

He laughed at that. "A week ago—it seems like years. A lot has happened in that time."

And the fact that those blue eyes of his pinned her let Lindsey know he included her in that. It warmed her to her bare toes, but she tried to ignore it.

"We can go back to Denver tomorrow," she continued. "I want to have another talk with Howard. And I think you should give some serious thought to the twins and the reality of taking them on permanently before we bring the authorities into this and you begin any kind of proceedings to keep them yourself."

He smiled at her. Calmly. Knowingly. As if he didn't need to think about it at all. Or maybe he already had.

But rather than addressing what she'd proposed he changed the subject. "You really are good at this."

"Don't sound so surprised."

He refilled both of their wine glasses and settled back from his finished meal to study her. "How did you go from doing social work to being a P.I., anyway?"

Lindsey could see that he'd heard all he wanted to about the situation with the twins and let the conversation flow naturally on. "I got tired of spending more time with paperwork than actually solving problems.

My brother Quinn had left the police force to open the agency and he asked me to join him. That was about three and a half years ago."

"How dangerous is it?"

She shrugged. "Not as dangerous as television makes it look. But I have been chased on occasion by people who were mad about being served a summons, and I've run into one or two situations that weren't nice. Still, though, for the most part the job is just what you've seen—legwork." She repeated the word she'd used earlier, but somehow this time, all on its own, it was slightly suggestive. Probably because it reminded her of Graham's appreciative glance at the pool.

He seemed to be remembering, too, because his smile was slow and sexy.

"I'd rather you'd said your work doesn't ever put you in jeopardy," he admitted. "The more I've gotten to know you this week, the more concerned I've been about it. Now that you're in my life I wouldn't want anything to take you out of it."

That unnerved her. Maybe because she didn't want anything to take her out of his life, either, which meant that somewhere along the way she'd actually come to feel that she was a part of that life.

She took her wine and stood, going to the balcony's railing to look down at the brook that ran through the manicured grounds below.

The quiet of the night was interrupted by the scrape of Graham's chair as he left the table, too, to come and stand beside her. But rather than looking out at the scenery, he leaned a hip against the railing and looked at her.

"Would it scare you if I told you that in spite of the short amount of time we've been together, I think I might be falling in—"

"Yes."

He laughed. "Okay. Then I won't say it." He bent over and whispered in her ear. "But it's true."

Her head tilted into the warmth of his breath against her skin, but as if the sensation didn't affect her, she said, "That's a lot more dangerous than being a P.I."

He raised a single index finger to brush her hair back from the sensitive hollow of her temple. "You could be right. Because when I start chasing you I won't stop until you're caught," he joked.

"Shall I try for a head start?" she bantered back, finally turning to face him.

He arched a brow at her and gave her a crooked grin. "Could be interesting."

Then he kissed her. Lightly, almost teasingly. And only once. "Can I at least say that I want you?"

A smile of her own came reflexively. "You just did."

"And would you say, 'I want you, too'?" This time he was definitely teasing.

"I want you, too," she repeated, as if she didn't actually mean it.

"With feeling."

"I want you, too, with feeling."

"Oh, good, because that's how you've got me," he countered between kisses. "You don't know how tough it was for me to leave you last night," he went on in a soft, husky timbre.

But she did know, because it had been every bit as tough for her the night before that. As tough as it would be now, even after just a few innocent kisses, to go to her room alone.

"I would never do anything to hurt you, Lindsey," he said between more kisses, though they were growing progressively longer, progressively deeper.

"And here I was worried about bruises," she answered with mild facetiousness.

"Definitely no bruises," he assured, kissing her again. "And no pressure, either."

Which meant she could say no to what was clearly happening between them. That if she did, he'd accept it and he wouldn't push what seemed to have been brewing every minute that they'd been together today. Maybe every minute they'd been together since they met.

No, if she rejected him he would back away from her and they'd spend the evening watching television or talking before going their separate ways to their separate beds, and he wouldn't say a word about it.

But tonight that voice of caution in her mind was still so quiet she could ignore it if she wanted to.

And she did want to.

Because she also wanted, at that moment, to be in Graham's arms. To have him make love to her. To know completely what she'd only tasted of, imagined, longed for.

She set her wine glass on the railing, glanced up at him and said, "Okay, I won't pressure you. But—"

He cut off her words with a laugh and another kiss, a longer one, lingering, his lips parted as he cradled the back of her head to hold her to it.

Warmly. Sweetly. Patiently. He kissed her as if he had all the time in the world. And yet it was enough to light sparks deep inside her.

He took her hand and led her along the balcony to the French doors of her room, opening them wide, but not taking her through them.

Instead he kissed her once more. "Let me love you," he whispered.

Her answer was to kiss him back and then to take the first step into her bedroom.

He didn't need more invitation than that.

He went in with her, going all the way to the bed to pull back the spread and blanket.

Then he reached to the bottom of his shirt with his arms x-ed over his flat belly, curling it up and over his head in one motion.

Lamplight threaded through his milk-chocolate-colored hair and christened his glorious shoulders and chest, and Lindsey thought she could have looked at him forever except that it would mean she couldn't touch him and she wanted to do that even more.

He came to her where she stood in the center of the room, stopping close in front of her. She raised her eyes slowly up from the center of his chest to his glorious, heart-stoppingly handsome face. She could smell the clean scent of his after-shave, feel the heat of him, and it all worked to make her knees turn to water.

He cupped her face in his palms, using his thumbs to smooth feathery strokes against her cheeks, so slowly, again and again, each stroke somehow more sensuous than the one before.

He lowered his mouth to hers once more in short, chaste meetings of his parted lips with hers, drawing her nearer.

She matched the fluid drifting of his mouth to and from hers, and her lips parted, too, as she wrapped her arms around his waist, laying her palms flat against his

lowest ribs, feeling the sleek texture of his flesh and bone as her hands glided up his back to his broad and hard shoulders.

His breathing grew heavier.

Or was it hers?

Both. It was both. Mingling and mixing and giving them away....

He hooked his thumbs in the elastic waistband of her shorts. His fingers rode the small curve of her derriere while the force of his arms held her possessively and the breadth of his shoulders curved around her.

She thought he was going to ease her shorts down. She wanted him to. But instead he went on kissing her, his tongue tracing the edges of her teeth, exploring, leisurely finding its way between, as his hands merely stayed riding her rump.

And then he pulled away, lifting her effortlessly to put her carefully on the bed where he took his place beside her, half his body pressed over half of hers while his mouth came back again, this time open wide and with a new hunger, a new urgency that sent his tongue thrusting forcefully, with the promise of what was to come.

She met and matched each thrust, each circling, feeling her own needs gathering, growing stronger, more demanding.

Needs that were clearly echoed in Graham for he suddenly drew himself away from her, kneeling on the mattress and pulling her up with him so that deft hands could slip beneath her tank top, easing it off. He kissed each inch of her flat stomach as it was exposed, freed her breasts to the air-conditioned coolness of the room, awakening her body to a heightened sensitivity.

His mouth found hers again, reclaiming it. He eased her back to the pillows. One heavy thigh crossed over her and he lowered the solid expanse of his chest to the naked softness of hers.

The first press of her tightened nipples to his warm skin sent a fresh surge of excitement through Lindsey, setting flame to what had only been sparks inside her before, emboldening her.

Her tongue met his, followed his retreat to test the inside of his mouth, all velvet and wet smoothness as her hands coursed up his naked back, filling themselves with the sleek tautness of his flesh.

But he distracted her with the feel of his fingers hooked into the front of her tennis shorts, this time sliding them lower as she'd wished for before.

A faint groan eased from her throat at the enticing thought of being completely free of clothes. But she didn't want to be alone in that and reached her own hands to the waistband button of his jeans, letting the backs of her fingers slip between the denim and his stomach.

His groan was deeper than hers as she unfastened that button, but she didn't go any further, instead teasing his flat middle with feather-light strokes of the backs of fingers that only threatened to go lower but never did.

He wasn't having much of that, though. He pushed her hands down just enough to spread his zipper before he slid from her side and off the bed to peel the jeans away, and for a moment she delighted in the view of him naked and more masculinely magnificent than she'd imagined.

But he didn't give her long to indulge in the sight before he knelt on the mattress again and reached for her

shorts, grasping her panties at the same time, and sliding them both off to leave her as naked as he was.

And as aroused, though the proof of hers wasn't as obvious. Or as incredible.

She reached her hands to his rippled stomach, fingers splayed, palms too timid to go where she wanted them to and so sliding upward until she reached the small nubs of his nipples.

Her back arched to him with no thought but that he was too far from her and she needed the feel of him more than the sight.

He moaned softly as her mouth sought his, her tongue tracing his upper lip.

Again he eased her to lie flat, partially covering her body with his, his thigh sliding over her lap, the evidence of his desire pushing insistently against her hip.

She felt his fingers glide up her stomach, the anticipation building in her until his palm took her breast at last, kneading, rolling her own taut bud between thumb and forefinger.

His mouth lowered, and his tongue teased circles around her nipple. Her shoulders drew back, thrusting her farther into his suckling mouth—pulling, drawing, nipping in gentle bites.

Her hands entwined in the coarseness of his hair, and her passions caught fire with the feel of his lips, his tongue, his teeth. . . .

That was when all inhibitions fled her. She needed to know him as intimately by touch as he knew her, and she set out to do that.

The skin of his sides, his back, his chest, his biceps, was taut and slippery, corded and bulging, rougher than hers in some places and satin smooth in others.

Her hands slid to his firm derriere, where only her eyes had feasted before, down hard thighs and then forward, hesitating for only a moment before sliding upward again until she found the shaft of rigid, hot silk.

Her first grasp brought a sharp gasp from him, and then a rumbling groan of pleasure and encouragement before he chuckled low in his throat, as if accepting a sensual challenge to match the flames she had ignited in him.

As his mouth still worked wonders at her breast, his hand ran lightly down her side. He found her legs just barely parted, and his teasing fingers carefully made their way between. Deeply between . . .

This time it was Lindsey who moaned, softly but almost in agony, she wanted him so much. She raised her hips against the heel of his hand and let her own grip tighten and move—up and down—until his passion seemed to ignite into flames too hot to endure, spurring him to nearly yank away from her, to rise above her, widening the gap between her knees to lower himself there in what might have been a lunge home had he not stopped in an act of self-control that almost seemed painful. Instead he came to her slowly, with great care.

Almost too much care, for she needed desperately to feel him fully inside her, and arched against him to tell him so.

And then he was fully inside her. Filling her, reaching to the core of her with that long, thick shaft that joined them together, body and soul.

For a moment he was perfectly still, as if letting her become accustomed to him. Then he pulsed, once, twice, a third time, tickling the very entrance to her womb, driving her wild with need, until finally, finally,

he began with a thrust that was so slow it was agony and bliss at the same time.

She flexed around him and answered that thrust and those that came after, but his urgency was as great as hers and like a train gaining speed, before long he was driving deeply within her, filling and easing, taking her step-by-step to climb higher and higher, faster and faster....

Lindsey clung to him, letting him carry her all the way to an explosive peak, crying out softly as wave after wave of pure ecstasy washed through her, prolonged by his own climb as he plunged into her, claiming her, possessing her, loving her....

He said her name in a groan of pure pleasure as his whole body tensed into one tight cord and he drove into her with the full power of his passion, so much so that it set off a second climax in her, too, taking her by surprise—unbelievable, sublime surprise.

And then, slowly, they both came back from the summit, totally spent. Satiated to the brink of exhaustion.

Everything came to a stop but their shallow breathing and racing pulses. Graham rested atop her, his glorious body weighing her into the mattress until those things quieted, too.

Then he rose on his forearms and lowered his mouth for three soft, lingering kisses that tasted of salt, before he left her to roll to his back, taking her with him so that she lay seamlessly against his side, her head in the bed of his shoulder, her thigh riding his.

"I love you," he whispered so softly it was as if he didn't mean for her to hear it.

But although she hadn't wanted to before, the words put a glimmer to the beauty of the act they'd just shared, sealing it.

And she suddenly realized that she could have answered with the same words and meant it, for somehow, even when she'd been fighting the hardest against it, falling in love with him was just what she'd done.

But she couldn't say it, for loving him was where the real danger in her life was. So instead she pressed a kiss to the spot on his chest just above his heart.

He cupped the back of her head with his big hand and guided her to rest again in the same spot as before, his fingers caressing her hair, keeping her there even as his other arm came around her.

And as she felt him relax and give in to sleep, the voice of caution made itself heard loud and clear again.

But she hushed it. For the moment at least.

Because even though there was much she needed to remember and protect herself from, right then none of it mattered.

The only thing that was important was that he was holding her, loving her....

And it all felt too wonderful to be bad.

Chapter Eight

"Wa mik."

It had been awhile since the sound of a child's voice had awakened Lindsey. Awhile since that awakening had occurred in a man's arms.

It felt good.

Then very disconcerting.

Then good again, albeit more cautiously, as she went from the pure pleasure of it, to a moment of confusion about how it could be happening and where she was, back to allowing herself to enjoy it when she remembered it was Graham who held her. In a hotel suite in Colorado Springs. With the twins in the next room.

Graham's arms tightened around her and he pressed a kiss to the top of her head. "Okay, so some things about having kids are damn inconvenient," he whispered as they both waited for any more sounds from the babies' room.

Keeping his arms around her, he rolled to his side to face her, swinging a divinely heavy masculine leg over her hip to bring their lower halves together, too. It left Lindsey with no doubt that there was something he'd rather be doing this morning than playing parent.

An instant, answering desire rose in her, but just as she wished an hour's more sleep on Kate and Charlie, she heard, "Mik!"

Graham groaned—a sound that mingled passion and something that sounded akin to pain. "There's no hope. Once they're awake we're done for," he said as if he'd read her thoughts.

But it was so comfortable there in that bed with the mattress and sheets cocooning them and Graham's big body entwined with hers—all sleek naked skin and a perfect meshing of soft curves, honed hollows and hard ridges—that Lindsey had to hope...

"Mik, Gam!"

"Charlie will chime in here any second."

"Gam?" the slightly lower of the two baby voices came, as if on cue.

Once more Graham moaned. But that was as far as his complaints went. He flexed against her, gave up whispering and said in a raspy, morning voice, "So, Ms. Sherlock, since we basically know what's going on with these two human alarm clocks—thanks to your expert deductions and investigations—what do you say to staying here in the Springs another day anyway and meeting me back in this bed during the morning nap time?"

A slow, involuntary smile spread Lindsey's lips as temptation overpowered her. She heard herself say, "Maybe if you twist my arm."

"Arm-twisting. Hand-holding. Neck nuzzling. Lip locking. Anything," he promised, pulsing his hips into hers and upping the ante in the temptation department. "A morning in bed. An afternoon sight-seeing. An evening swimming to tire out the twins. And then

another whole night right here....'' He reached a hand to her bare derriere and pulled her up tightly to him.

"Mmm," she murmured. And yet the arguments against such a blissful prospect began to raise their ugly heads in her mind. "I don't know, maybe we shouldn't," she hedged, knowing there were no maybes about it.

But rather than debate it, he began to trail kisses from her earlobe down the side of her neck—doing some of that nuzzling he'd mentioned—then on to her shoulder, down her arm, finding one small spot at the side of her breast that was peeking out from above the covers, and not only kissing her there, too, but giving a devil's flick of his tongue to boot.

The arguments receded as a brand-new craving emerged in her, hot and strong and more demanding than anything rational.

What was one day of indulgence out of her whole life, anyway?

"Wa mik." Kate's whine warned of much worse to come.

"Gam?" Charlie asked as if he were afraid Graham might not be there at all.

"Those are danger sounds. All hell will break loose if they aren't answered," Graham informed her. Then he kissed her quickly one last time and tore himself away. "Midmorning. Right back here," he ordered, pointing at the spot he'd just left so reluctantly.

Lindsey couldn't resist drinking in the sight of his gloriously naked body just before he dragged on the jeans he'd shucked the night before, zipping the zipper but leaving the waistband button open—clearly for comfort, unaware of just how tantalizing it was.

"Midmorning," she heard herself confirm.

Then she waited until he'd left the room, slipped out of bed and threw on her bathrobe so she could follow him and help with the twins.

The sooner they were taken care of, the sooner she'd have Graham to herself again.

And the sooner she'd get just one more taste of bliss.

BEST LAID PLANS . . .

Midmorning did not find Lindsey back in Graham's arms at all. Instead she, Graham, Kate and Charlie were in the car on their way home to Denver.

A frantic phone call from Annie at nine o'clock canceled the option of the leisurely day they had planned.

It seemed that Annie had gone to Graham's house for her regular day of cleaning and discovered the place had been broken into again.

But this time two babies in the middle of the bedroom floor were not what she'd come upon.

The house had been vandalized.

Furniture had been overturned, glass had been broken, televisions and the stereo had been destroyed and the bed in the master room had been sliced to ribbons, along with many of Graham's clothes in the closet.

But the most unsettling of all was a note stabbed to the kitchen table with a butcher's knife.

Leave Lori Alone or I'll Make You Sorry, it began.

And worse than that, it went on to threaten the babies.

WEARING HIS police uniform, Logan was already sitting in his car in front of the Springers' place as Lindsey and Graham drove up that afternoon. They'd surveyed the damage at Graham's home, read the note and then left the twins with the housekeeper when Gra-

ham had insisted on making one final visit to the residence of the woman he'd been involved with two years ago.

"I still don't think this is wise," Lindsey cautioned. "Marv Springer is a loose cannon when it comes to you. Confronting a person like that is not only dangerous, it usually doesn't do any good. You should just let Logan and me handle this."

Graham pulled up into the drive as far as the closed gate allowed. "A P.I. and a cop—that's hardly conciliatory. The bottom line here, Lindsey, is that this time I am responsible for stirring up dirt in this relationship, and I think I at least owe an explanation."

"We didn't do anything unreasonable. Tying the twins to Lori Springer when they turned up with your same blood type was the logical thing to do."

"I know, but on the chance that a little simple information and an apology from me will put an end to this, I think it's worth a shot."

Logan had gotten out of his car and was at the open driver's side window by then. Lindsey introduced her brother and Graham.

When they'd exchanged amenities and shaken hands, Logan glanced around Graham to Lindsey. "You just want me here for decoration, is that right?"

"Basically. I'm hoping that in the presence of a cop this guy will practice some self-control, but we want it unofficial so questions aren't raised about the twins just yet. Plus, you'll have a better chance of getting us through the gate," she said with a laugh at tactics she'd never have used were the cop in question not her brother.

Logan didn't seem to mind. He nodded. "Okay. Let's get to it then."

He turned to the speaker, pushing a button that brought the thickly accented voice of the woman who had allowed Lindsey and Graham in on the previous visit. Only this time Logan said a terse "Police, ma'am, please open up" and that did the trick.

Marv Springer was walking up from the tennis courts when the three of them drove to the front of the house. His racket was propped on his shoulder and he had a towel draped around his neck even though his all-white shorts and shirt showed no signs of sweat.

One look in the direction of his visitors, and the racket went slowly down to his side. "Get the hell off my property, Dunn!" he screamed.

So much for self-control in the presence of a police officer, Lindsey thought.

"We need to talk, Marv," Graham informed him patiently as he, Lindsey and Logan walked up to Springer.

"Yeah? Talk this!"

Before anyone realized what was going to happen, Marv Springer swung the tennis racket at Graham's head, catching him just above the temple.

All at once Logan and Lindsey both lunged forward, but Logan reached Springer first, tackling him onto the manicured lawn.

Seeing it, Lindsey turned back to Graham in a hurry. But he was all right, he hadn't even been knocked down. He was just trying to contend with the blood that was gushing down the side of his face.

"Dammit, Marv, I only came to clear things up," he told the other man with contained rancor in his tone as he accepted a wad of tissues Lindsey took from her purse and pressed it against the wound.

Logan let Springer get up when he stopped struggling but kept hold of his arm behind his back. "Are you sure you don't want me to arrest this guy?" he asked Graham.

"No, don't arrest him. Not this time, anyway," Graham answered disgustedly. He took a breath, apparently to hang on to his patience, and addressed Springer. "Look, there's no reason for me to beat around the bush. We found out the truth about the twins—they aren't mine and Lori's. I'm sorry the whole thing had to come up, but it's over now."

"It was over for you with Lori a long time ago. The better man won and you can't stand it. But I'm not sitting around while you pull some stupid prank to break us up again. This is only the beginning. I'm going to send you running with your tail between your legs before I'm through."

Still Graham remained calm. "Consider my not having you locked up for what you've done so far as my way of calling it even for bothering the two of you. But do anything else, Marv, and I will let them put you away for it."

"Nobody's going to put me anywhere. You think I can't do what I say I can and get away with it?" He threw a nod over his shoulder in Logan's direction. "Ask this pretty boy here if the right butter in the right palm doesn't fix things for people like me."

"Will you just listen to what I'm saying?" Graham's voice was rising.

"No, you listen to me," Springer shouted back. "I know you're using those brats as an excuse to come around Lori again, to force her to go to your place—yeah, I know about that. I followed her so she had to tell me what you were up to. And don't think I won't

come after you just because you have a couple of kids around, either. They get in my way and they'll go down, too."

"This is useless," Lindsey pointed out quietly.

Graham nodded, finally accepting that. Still, to Springer he said, "Don't be a jerk. Just forget this whole thing and go on with your life."

Springer started to spew more schoolyard-bully threats, but Graham turned away from him. "Let's get out of here," he said to Lindsey.

She glanced at Logan, who urged them to leave while he was still keeping Marv contained. "I think Mr. Springer and I should have a talk," he said.

Lindsey was thinking more about getting that cut on Graham's head looked at, so she left Logan to it.

GRAHAM REJECTED the idea of going to the hospital emergency room and instead insisted they just go back to his place. Most of the bleeding had stopped by the time they got there, but he was still a sight that made Annie gasp when they walked into the living room, where the twins were playing as the housekeeper wound up the cord for the vacuum cleaner.

"Boo-boo?" Kate asked sympathetically, going to Graham's side.

But Charlie didn't join his sister. He recoiled at the blood that stained Graham's face and shirtfront, and said, "Ooo-icky."

"Ooo-icky is right," Graham answered with a laugh. "I need to clean up," he added, disappearing down the hall with Kate following behind on her penguin's waddle as if she'd be of assistance.

"What happened?" Annie asked as she put the vacuum in a closet and took refuge on one corner of the

sofa, where her knitting bag and purse had apparently been left when she'd come in. She pulled her latest project into her lap and began working without seeming to think about it, as if she needed an outlet for this newest reason to be unnerved.

"Graham isn't hurt as badly as it looks," Lindsey answered the older woman, going on to fill her in briefly on the events with Springer.

But even though she soft-pedaled through it, Annie's knitting needles clicked faster and faster as she went along. By the time Lindsey was finished, the older woman had added about two inches to a tiny pink thing that looked like it was probably going to be a sweater for Kate.

Graham came back into the room then, carrying the little girl. One glance at his housekeeper seemed to alert him to the fact that she needed some reassurance. "Kate kissed it and made it better," he said, as if the whole incident didn't amount to a hill of beans.

"Maybe you should see a doctor," Annie said, fretting in spite of it.

"The cut isn't even bleeding anymore," Graham said by way of rejecting that idea. "A doctor would shave my head and stitch it for no good reason."

The doorbell rang just then and that seemed to end the discussion.

Lindsey went to answer it, finding Logan on the porch. "Is anything wrong?" she asked as she let him in, surprised to see him.

"You mean anything else?" he answered facetiously, nodding a hello to Graham as he stepped into the living room.

Graham introduced Annie and the twins, and when that was accomplished Lindsey rephrased her question. "Did something more happen after we left?"

"No," Logan admitted. "But I didn't have any better luck getting through to Springer than you did, Graham. In fact, Lori came home before I left and he wouldn't even listen to her when she tried to tell him to leave well enough alone. I just thought I'd better make sure you hadn't changed your mind about pressing charges."

Graham shook his head. "I think the threats are idle. Springer sees himself as a big man, so of course he had to put on a big show for everybody. But now that he knows I don't have any reason to contact Lori again, and that the kids aren't hers—because let's face it, he's probably been pretty crazy wondering if they really were and she'd just kept it hidden from him—he'll back off."

"He broke into your home," Logan reminded. "And when he saw you today, even with me standing right there, he hit you. Those are signs of someone who isn't hesitant to act."

"Actually I'm betting that it's just reaction to what's been going on and it'll end here because he won't have anything else to react to."

It was Annie who put in her two cents' worth then. "What about the babies? You wouldn't want him coming here with them in the house."

But that, too, Graham discounted. "Marv Springer made the same kind of threats at the end of the relationship with Lori two years ago. He was going to ruin Dunnit Tennis Shoes, he was going to be laying in wait for me late some night when I least expected it—things like that. Nothing came of any of it. Yes, this time he's

acted rashly, too, but I honestly think we've seen the last of it.''

Logan shrugged his concession to that. ''If Springer saw Lori come here and she told him some story about being forced, he was bound to respond. And slugging you today could have been basically bravado. If you've heard things like this before and he didn't follow through, odds are it's mostly hot air again now. And I did make it clear I'd arrest him if anything else happens, whether you pressed charges or not.''

''Plus I'll be especially cautious,'' Graham assured them all. ''I'll leave the ground lights on all night, make certain everything is locked up tight. And if there's even a hint of Marv Springer anywhere around, I'll call the police.''

Logan gave him a few last warnings—among them to notify the authorities if the phone or electricity suddenly went out. Then he said his goodbyes and left.

Annie had gathered her things to go by that time, too, but she hesitated before actually doing it. ''Would you like me to stay all night, just in case?'' she offered tentatively.

Graham patted her shoulder and thanked her for her concern even as he declined. ''The twins and I will be fine.''

She seemed glad he hadn't taken her up on the offer, and Lindsey was sure the older woman would be happy to get to her own home and lock the door behind her after this day.

''I'll see you all tomorrow,'' Annie said, heading down the hall to go out the kitchen door and leaving Lindsey alone with Graham and the twins.

''Spending the night with my housekeeper is not what I was hoping for,'' he said when he was sure Annie was

gone. "But if my P.I. wanted to stay, that would be a whole different story."

The cut on his head was beginning to swell, but it didn't detract from how appealing he was all cleaned up in his fresh white shirt and jeans. And though staying was just what Lindsey wanted to do, she knew it wasn't a good idea.

"Did you want me here in a professional capacity? As your bodyguard?" she asked, because she wanted to be sure about the situation.

He laughed, a throaty, sexy sound, as he came across the room to face her. He clasped his hands around her waist and pulled her so that their hips nudged together while he glanced down at her. "I want you. And your body. But in a professional capacity as a guard? That's not what I had in mind, no. I was thinking more along the lines of taking up where our plans for today left off."

She knew it probably didn't make any sense, and since she'd agreed to it earlier, he'd no doubt think she'd gone crazy to renege now, but somehow being back here had made the voice of caution in her mind pretty commanding again. Spending the night in his house, his bed, with the twins in the next room and all of them tucked in like one big, happy family, seemed like exactly what she shouldn't be doing. Not if she knew what was good for her.

"If you're sure you're okay here alone, I think maybe I'd better go home. I haven't been there since yesterday, you know. And I'd like to get over to talk to Howard Douglas early tomorrow—"

He kissed her to stop the onslaught of excuses. A slow, tender kiss that reminded her why she'd agreed that morning to more romps with him. It invited her to

relax, to remember how good things could be between them, to ignore that voice....

Her eyes drifted closed. Her head eased back as he deepened the kiss. And for a moment she let the magic of it carry her away.

But only for a moment before the fact that she liked it much too much reminded her to put the brakes on.

She eased away from it.

"This is all happening so fast, Graham," she said by way of explanation.

"And it terrifies you. I know." He kissed her again, just a brief peck, but even that was enough to light sparks in her bloodstream.

She tried to ignore them. "I need to be careful. You need to be careful. Your life is in an uproar right now. Mine...well, mine has just stopped being in one. Maybe we aren't thinking straight. Maybe we aren't seeing things clearly. Maybe—"

He kissed her yet again. "We'd have spent tonight together in Colorado Springs."

And the image of *how* they would have spent it kicked a hole in her resolve.

Still, she repaired it with some effort and held her ground. "But we aren't in Colorado Springs and I just can't stay the night here and play house."

She didn't know if the way she'd put that struck him as harsh or if it just put a different spin on what he was proposing, but he didn't kiss her this time. Instead he stopped the persuasion of his lips and looked down at her solemnly, seriously. "I'm not playing at anything, Lindsey."

"Neither am I. That's the trouble," she heard herself admit before she'd even considered the wisdom of it. But it was true. Graham, her feelings for him, her

growing attachment to the twins—in spite of every attempt to keep herself emotionally removed from them—none of it was a game. It was all getting very serious. And she didn't think it should be. Not now. Not so soon. Not so quickly.

"I need to sort through what's happening, what I'm feeling. We both need to be a lot more careful than we've been," she repeated. "And I can't just stay here."

She pushed out of his arms while she could still force herself to, straightened her shoulders and put on her best businesslike face before glancing at him again.

So handsome. So big. So sexy. So terrific. And all there for her if only—

She crushed the thought.

"If you don't think you need me on the job tonight—"

"I need you in a lot of ways—I want you in a lot of ways—but on the job is not one of them," he said. Then, with a quirky half smile he added, "Although I should get points for not using *the job* as an excuse to keep you here so I can work at breaking down your resistance."

"Okay, points given," she answered, appreciating his lightening of the tone she'd ended with.

"Are you sure you wouldn't at least consider staying for dinner, though? Whatever Annie left in the oven smells pretty good."

He sounded like the wolf tempting Red Riding Hood, and Lindsey couldn't resist laughing at him. But still she didn't waver. "I don't think so. I really do need some time . . . some space."

And before she could change her mind, she took her purse and her overnight bag and headed for the door.

But as she was about to go out, the sound of Graham's voice reached her. "There's just one thing, Lindsey."

She glanced back at him, raising her eyebrows in question.

"You should know that we can try to slow down what's happening here, but I can't stop it."

Maybe neither could she.

"And I don't want to," he added.

Maybe neither did she.

Which was exactly what scared her.

But she didn't say that. Instead she said, "I'll be here after I talk to your uncle in the morning."

"Or if you change your mind in the middle of the night—don't even hesitate to come back."

"If somebody shows up here in the middle of the night you'd better think it's Marv Springer and call the cops."

He rolled his eyes at her. "Okay, so let me know you're coming and *then* don't even hesitate."

The power of suggestion was strong, and she knew she was going to spend the whole night now fighting the urge to do just that.

But fighting it was just what she'd do because she needed to think about everything that was going on— inside her, and between her and Graham—and that couldn't be done when she was so overwhelmed by all that was aroused when she was anywhere near him.

"Lock your doors, Graham," she said with a smile, and then she left.

GRAHAM HAD INSOMNIA that night. But Marv Springer's threats didn't have anything to do with it.

It was Lindsey who was on his mind. Wanting her with him. In his bed.

By midnight he'd picked up the phone a half dozen times to call her, but so far he hadn't gone through with it. He kept hanging up middial, telling himself to give her the time and space she needed.

It couldn't be easy for her, he knew, to find herself getting involved with someone so soon after her divorce and at a pace that would make anyone's head spin. And the fact that there might well be kids included in the equation to remind her of Bobby and losing him couldn't help matters, either. He acknowledged all of that.

And she was probably right—he should be careful, too.

It was risky business to fall in love with someone so fresh from a serious relationship.

He should know. Lori Springer had been in a similar situation when he'd met her.

Not that Lindsey was hiding an estranged husband in the background or keeping any of her past a secret. But there was still baggage and he knew it.

He'd meant it when he'd said there was nothing about his feelings for her or their relationship that he was playing at, though. Because risky business or not, he really was in love with her.

And that couldn't be stopped or turned off or even slowed down just because the timing was lousy.

The real question for him, he thought, was whether Lindsey was free of her past, unlike Lori Springer. Emotionally free.

That made him think about all he'd witnessed at her house on Sunday as she'd said goodbye to her former stepson.

She'd said at the time that she wasn't saying good-bye to her ex-husband, that everything between them was in the past, over with. And when Graham re-hashed in his mind what had gone on that day, he real-ized he believed her.

There'd been no signs of affection for Dave Morrisy, no lingering glances, not even an overly exaggerated show of contempt that spoke of a bond still existing between them.

And Graham hadn't sensed anything more subtle, either, though he thought he would have if Lindsey were carrying a torch for the other man.

No, her heart might still be a little ragged around the edges, but Graham honestly believed she was free of her past. Free to have a future with him.

A future he wanted to start right this minute.

He picked up the phone yet again and dialed six digits of her phone number.

But he paused before punching in that last one.

She needed some time.

She needed some space.

She needed to come to grips with moving on with her life.

Once more he hung up without completing the call.

He loved her too much to rush her. Too much to pressure her.

And he trusted her, too, he realized. Trusted that she'd come around to accepting that she loved him, the same way he loved her—because he believed she did—and that they belonged together no matter how fast it happened.

So he would woo her. Court her. Seduce her....

Well, maybe that wasn't such a good idea. For he knew that not only couldn't he rush her or pressure her,

but that he also shouldn't overwhelm her by proving with passion that something pretty powerful was at work here.

She had to realize it on her own, and he had to wait for her to do it.

No matter how tough that might be for him.

And in the meantime, he'd just love her, take a lot of cold showers and hope like hell it didn't take her too long.

Chapter Nine

"The babies are gone!"

It took Lindsey a moment for Graham's words to sink in. After all, it was hardly what she'd expected to hear when she answered the phone at eight the next morning.

"What do you mean the babies are gone?" she asked.

"Just what I said. I had insomnia last night and I guess when I finally fell asleep it must have been pretty deep. I didn't hear a thing and I didn't wake up until a few minutes ago. I couldn't figure out why the twins hadn't been screaming for their milk, and the reason is that sometime while I was in that deep sleep and not hearing anything, Kate and Charlie were kidnapped."

"Was the house broken into again?"

"No. Springer smashed a vase in his rampage. I had some spare house keys in it. All I can figure is that he must have realized what they were and taken one of them to let himself in if he wanted to come back and do more damage or make good on his threats."

Tension mixed with anger made Graham sound like a powder keg about to explode.

Lindsey kept her voice calm, even though she was feeling anything but. "Have you searched for the twins?

Maybe they discovered how to climb out of the crib and they've crawled into a cupboard or a closet.''

"They're not here, Lindsey. And you know they couldn't get out of the house by themselves. I'm telling you, Springer took the key, snuck in sometime after two this morning, snatched them and snuck back out. And I'm going after them."

"Graham, wait—" Something about this didn't feel right but Lindsey couldn't put her finger on it.

"I'm not waiting. This is my fault. I should have had that bastard locked up."

Lindsey could tell that Graham was too mad and worried to reason with, and she felt an urgency herself that made her ignore her instincts. "I'll meet you at the Springers' gate. Sit tight until I get there."

"Just get there," he ordered without agreeing to wait for her. Then he hung up.

Lindsey had had her morning shower before Graham's call but she wasn't dressed yet. The moment she let go of the phone, she dropped her bathrobe where she stood and threw on the first pair of jeans and T-shirt she reached in the nearest drawer, not caring what it was she was putting on, thinking only of Kate and Charlie and Graham.

Lord, she hadn't believed Springer would actually do anything to the kids. It had been Graham she'd feared for, and she'd honestly felt that the threats against Kate and Charlie had only been for effect.

Three swipes of a brush was all she gave her hair before she grabbed her purse and made a dash through the house to her car in the garage.

But as she backed out of the driveway, that sense that something about this was not quite right struck again.

Why would Springer kidnap the twins? He knew they didn't belong to Lori and he hadn't wanted her anywhere around them. So why take them?

Unless he meant to dispose of them....

No, that thought was too horrible. And even Marv Springer wasn't bad enough to harm two innocent babies.

But taking the twins was a good way to get back at Graham for whatever stress Lindsey's investigation had caused Marv. It was a possibility.

And yet it still didn't feel right for some reason.

Maybe because taking the kids was a much bigger deal than vandalism or hitting Graham with a tennis racket. Would Springer go so far as to commit a federal crime that he would not be able to buy his way out of under any circumstances?

Lindsey had her doubts.

But if Marv Springer didn't take the kids, who did? she asked herself, still headed for the Springers' place.

Was it possible Norris Planter had had a change of heart and come back for them?

That didn't seem plausible, either. From all reports, he hadn't felt much of a bond with Kate or Charlie. And he'd been afraid of being accused of neglect or abuse. Certainly he'd know that abandoning them for a week and then kidnapping them back wouldn't make the authorities look more kindly on him.

And why retrieve two kids he'd broken into Graham's house to get rid of in the first place?

Unless he wasn't the one to leave the babies with Graham.

What if he'd left them with Howard—the "family in Denver" he'd mentioned. What if Howard had left

Kate and Charlie with Graham and for some reason had now taken them back?

But that seemed even more unlikely as, in her mind's eye, she saw the tiny old man, moving at his slow, shuffling pace, his clothes hanging on his frail form as if there were only bones inside them.

"Oh my God," Lindsey suddenly whispered as she realized what it was that was niggling at her.

But was it possible?

Horns honked as she swerved in front of two lanes of highway traffic to the next exit.

"It isn't Springer, Graham. It isn't Springer," she chanted to herself as if the message might reach him as she searched the side streets for a pay phone.

When she spotted one, she turned into the convenience store parking lot so fast her tires squealed, then squealed again as she slammed on her brakes in front of it.

She tore through her purse to find her tablet, flipping through the pages on her way to the booth.

And while she punched in the numbers to Graham's cellular phone, she prayed she could reach him before he barged in on Marv Springer.

Because the Springers were not who needed to be barged in on.

The man with the answers—if not the twins—was Howard Douglas.

"LINDSEY, I THINK you've lost your mind," Graham told her when they'd both parked in front of his uncle's house and left their respective cars to head up the walk.

"Then why are you here?" she challenged.

"Because you sounded so sure. But Howard? How could he possibly—"

Lindsey had told Graham nothing of what she suspected and only insisted he meet her at his uncle's house rather than the Springers'. Even now she didn't fill him in but only cut off his words to say, "Unless I miss my guess, your uncle knows a lot more than he told us. And until I have what I'm thinking confirmed, I don't want to go up another blind alley."

"And in the meantime Kate and Charlie—"

"Are perfectly safe. Safer than they were at your place," she told him with complete confidence as she rang the doorbell.

After a slightly extended wait for the old man, Howard Douglas finally opened the door. His expression was curious for a moment and then serenely pleased to see them.

"Graham! I didn't expect you to visit again so soon. And you've brought the lady detective. How nice."

"We need to talk to you, Howard," Graham answered the greeting.

"Glad for the company," the elderly gentleman assured them as he ushered them in.

He wore the same clothes he'd had on when they'd been there before—a green cardigan over a plaid flannel shirt and brown dress pants—making Lindsey wonder if he owned anything else. And they still hung so loosely on him that they looked as though they belonged to a bigger man.

"Come on into the living room," he urged, shuffling in that direction himself.

The new color television Graham had sent was playing a morning news show. Howard used the remote

control on the table near his recliner to mute the sound and waved them to the couch before he sat in his chair.

"What's on your mind?" he asked Graham.

But it was Lindsey who answered. "Tell us about Graham's mother, Mr. Douglas."

"What would you like to know?"

"Where she took Kate and Charlie." Lindsey stared at the old man, who was suddenly stone-statue still, but nothing showed in his expression.

"My mother?" Graham asked, and though Lindsey didn't look at him she knew he'd turned to her in surprise. "What are you talking about?"

Lindsey didn't answer him directly. Instead she spoke to his uncle. "That's who Annie is, isn't she?"

"Excuse me?" the old man finally said.

Lindsey nodded at his sweater. "It took me until just a little while ago to put two and two together. But the day I met Graham's housekeeper, she was knitting that green sweater you're wearing—the same sweater you had on the last time Graham and I were here." Lindsey finally looked at Graham. "The 'family in Denver' who Norris planter was bringing the babies to wasn't you or your uncle. It was your mother—Annie. Francine was her name, right? She was probably called Frannie. Knock off a couple of letters and she became Annie."

Graham's blue eyes bored into Lindsey as he seemed to be assimilating all of this and trying to decide if it could possibly be true.

The process was cut short when Annie stepped through the swinging door that led to the kitchen.

And just beyond, the twins were tied with towels around their waists to two chairs at the table, eating jelly-slathered toast.

Annie stood frozen in the doorway, and Graham's gaze went from Lindsey to his housekeeper almost in slow motion.

"Annie?" he said, the simple name laden with questions, with demands for explanations, for confirmation.

"She's right," the older woman admitted quietly, fearfully.

"Why don't you come in and sit down and tell us about it?" Lindsey invited, unsure herself what Graham's reaction was going to be when the shock wore off.

Annie glanced over her shoulders at the twins, but they were content to be licking the jelly off their toast and subsequently smearing it all over their faces, oblivious to what was playing out in the living room.

"I'll watch over the kids," Howard offered. Pushing himself from his chair, he patted Annie's shoulder reassuringly, easing her out of the doorway so he could go through it and close the door after himself.

But Annie only moved a few feet into the room and she didn't sit. She went on standing as if she were facing a firing squad.

"I know you believed I was dead," she said to Graham. "I know that's what your father told you. It was what he wished were true, I suppose."

Graham watched the woman he'd thought to be only his housekeeper, but Lindsey couldn't tell anything from his face and she wondered if he was ever going to speak.

Finally he said, "Why? How...?"

"Obviously you know I wasn't faithful to your father. All these years I'd hoped you were too young to

remember. But then you told Lindsey the whole thing—even about the pregnancy."

"And that you left to be with the other man," Graham added, completing the picture.

"Your father and I weren't happy together. We weren't suited for one another. And I fell in love with someone else. When I realized I was pregnant with Charmayne I couldn't let your father believe the baby was his. I had to tell him the truth. But in all I'd imagined, I'd never thought he'd respond as vindictively as he did. I never even considered that he might not let me have you."

"He wouldn't *let* you have me?" Graham repeated.

Lindsey knew that the dubious note in his voice was put there by years of believing his mother hadn't wanted him. In fact, knowing both of these people made it excruciating to witness the pain they were suffering at that moment for things that had happened over thirty years ago.

"I tried, Graham. I tried," Annie said, her tone begging him to believe her. "Courts and lawyers and . . . I tried. But times were different then. I was an adulteress." The word seemed so foul to the taste that she could barely endure having it in her mouth.

She swallowed with some difficulty and then went on. "And your father was an appellate judge. He was a well-respected man with prestige, with friends in high places, and, worse than that, associates in lower places."

"What does that mean?" Graham asked of what seemed to hold significance for her.

The older woman shrugged. "He had the power to overturn other judges' verdicts on appeal. Those who heard our case risked his wrath in the future if they de-

cided in my favor instead of his. But still, I took it as far as I could. The legal battle was ugly, and when it was over, not only did I lose total custody of you, the ruling was that I was unfit to be around you at all, that I was an immoral, corrupting influence. I wasn't to have any contact with you whatsoever." There was still bitterness over that turn of events and it made her lower lip quiver as if the decision had been handed down only recently.

Lindsey's heart went out to Annie, who had experienced just what Lindsey had with Bobby, only Annie's loss had been of a child she'd given birth to.

"What about that one time I saw you just after I started school?" Graham asked. "Was that before or after the ruling?"

Her eyes welled with tears but she didn't let them fall. "After. I'd spent months and months abiding by the court orders while I worked through legal channels. But it didn't matter. In the end I still lost you. I couldn't stand it. I couldn't stand not seeing you, not being a mother to you, so I decided to sneak. But your father found out and he had me arrested and put in jail. I spent ten days in a women's correctional facility. After that I was too afraid..." Her voice dwindled off apologetically.

It took her a moment before she was able to go on. "I kept track of you, though—at a distance so you wouldn't see me. But I was there watching you play with your friends as often as I could arrange it. I saw you learning to drive a car, at your first job, with some of the girls you liked. I was at your graduations from high school and college. I was even at the opening of Dunnit Tennis Shoes."

"Why didn't you approach me once I'd grown up?"

"By then I was afraid it was too late. I knew you believed I was dead, and after all that time I didn't think you'd just welcome me with open arms."

"So you came to work for me instead."

"I suppose this sounds crazy, but I couldn't stay away any longer. I lost my husband last year to a heart attack, and then Charmayne and Francine died just two months later... Death comes in threes, isn't that what they say? All at once everyone close to me was gone. Everyone except the twins. But they were left with Norris Planter." She said the name with revulsion, her expression giving further evidence of her dislike of the man.

"He and I never got along," she explained. "He's a no-good, lazy drunk. After the accident I went to Colorado Springs to see what was going to happen to Kate and Charlie, but they weren't at the house, and he told me he'd found out who their father was, that he'd given them to him and that they weren't even in Colorado anymore. He said I didn't have any reason to bother him ever again. I guess that was the point of his lying to me." She breathed a disgusted sigh and shook her head. "Maybe I shouldn't have believed him, but I was in such a bad way at the time, and it wasn't as if he'd ever been a doting grandfather. I honestly thought Kate and Charlie were gone, too."

"And that left me."

Her eyes beseeched him. "Don't say it as if you were a last resort, Graham. I was always desperate to be with you, but I'd tried to soothe it with my spy missions to the sidelines of your life, and having the rest of my family helped dull the pain. But suddenly there was nothing and no one left as a buffer for it. Then I read that article about you, and that offhand mention that

you were in the market for a housekeeper was like a sign
to me that there was a way for me to be near you. I
thought that I'd changed enough after so many years
that you wouldn't recognize me, and I decided that
working for you, even if I had to pretend to be someone else, would at least let me see you, let me care for
you, let me finally be a part of your life."

Howard pushed open the door to the kitchen just
then and held it for Kate and Charlie to penguin-walk
through. They spotted Graham and went right to him
as if seeing him there was a happy surprise for them.

Somehow it eased the tension in the room.

Graham scooped them up to hold one on each knee
and kissed them both on the top of their downy heads.
"And what about these two?" he asked with a challenge still in his voice.

"Norris hadn't found out who their father was or
given them up. It seems that until a month or so ago his
having the twins had spurred a pretty powerful sympa-
thy element among his neighbors. It had been garnering him a lot of help—financial and otherwise. But he'd
reaped all the benefits he could and so he brought them
to me."

Annie seemed to pause to take in the sight of her son
cuddling her great-grandchildren, and one look at the
love in her eyes for all three of them made Lindsey
wonder how the older woman had ever managed to hide
it before this.

"I was glad to have them, they're such good babies," she said. "But I'm sixty-seven years old, Graham. I may not live long enough to see them all grown
up and on their own."

"And they're a handful. She just can't keep up with
them," Howard added as if he knew she wouldn't ad-

mit it herself. "Plus babies are expensive. When they got here they both had ear infections, and one trip to the doctor set her back over a hundred dollars. A fixed income can't withstand that, not even when it's supplemented."

"I just couldn't care for them properly in any way," Annie went on before Howard could say more. "And there you were, Graham. Such a good man—kind and patient and generous. I knew the right place for them was with you, that you would be a wonderful father to them. And if they were with you I'd still be able to see them and help with them so you wouldn't have the complete burden, but still they could be raised the way they deserve to be, and…well, and so I made it look as if someone had broken in, and Howard and I left them in your bedroom," she finished very quietly.

"Then why take them back last night?" he asked.

"I read the note left by that man who vandalized your house. And then he actually did hit you. I was afraid to leave all three of you there when he might show up at any minute and make good on his threats. There was nothing I could do or say to get you out of harm's way, but I just couldn't leave Kate and Charlie. Not only were they in danger. I knew if they were with you, you'd defend them before taking care of yourself. I had to at least free you from that, so Howard and I watched for your lights to go out last night and then used my key to come in and take them."

And Howard seemed pretty pleased with himself to have been able to help.

"I'm surprised the twins didn't show any recognition of you," Lindsey said to Annie.

"I've worried about that. But they're so friendly to everyone, I guess it was just hard to tell when they did

know someone and when they didn't. I think it's been more difficult for me not to show anything. I've had to be so careful not to dote on them.''

And that seemed to be that.

Lindsey didn't have anything else to ask, and apparently neither did Graham because silence fell then and tension hung in the air. It was all up to him. Acceptance or rejection. Warmth or recriminations. A beginning or an end.

He looked from Kate to Charlie. From Howard to the woman he knew as Annie. And Lindsey thought he had to be torn between old hurts and resentments and a woman whom he'd grown genuinely fond of in the past few months.

Then he took a deep breath and sighed it out. "Well, it seems like we have a lot of catching up to do, don't we? Not to mention a few Mother's Days to make up for.''

A sob escaped Annie, who pressed both hands over her mouth as tears gathered in her eyes again and this time coursed down her cheeks.

"Good boy!'' Howard cheered from the sidelines.

Graham chuckled, set the twins on the floor and crossed to his mother, wrapping her in a hug she melted into.

And that was when Lindsey knew her work was finished and she didn't belong there anymore.

So she slipped out of the house and left the family to its reunion.

IT WAS AFTER THREE in the afternoon when Graham came to Lindsey's house. He was by himself and, unlike earlier that morning when he'd looked as if he'd dived into the nearest clothes at hand, now his appear-

ance showed some care in the khaki slacks and bright yellow polo shirt he wore.

Lindsey had changed from what she'd had on earlier, too, into shorts and a V-necked T-shirt that were cooler for weeding the flower boxes that lined the front foundation of her house.

She tried not to be thrilled that he'd come, especially not after spending the time since leaving him lecturing herself that now that the case was solved, her relationship with him should be ended, too. But she was thrilled just the same.

"Hey, lady, I have a bone to pick with you," he greeted, not sounding in the least angry.

He sat on the edge of the low brick wall that formed her flower boxes.

Lindsey went from her knees to sit beside him. "Yeah? What'd I do wrong?" she said, posturing like one bully facing another.

"You disappeared when my back was turned and my hands were full."

"I thought a little private time was in order."

"Which was not a reason for you to leave."

"Seemed like it was. I'd done my job."

He took her hand and pulled off the gardening glove she wore to entwine her bare fingers with his. "That's what I was afraid of."

"What?"

"That you were figuring now that you'd finished working for me, we'd just call everything quits."

She only shrugged her admission of that very thing and changed the subject. "How do things stand with you and your mother, and the twins?"

"I had a lot to take in. You could have warned me a little ahead of time that you'd realized who Annie was."

"Like I said, I wanted some confirmation before leading you up another blind alley. Besides, I only realized it myself on the way to the Springers' place. But you haven't answered my question. What's happening on the family front?"

This time it was Graham who shrugged. "Looks like I just gained one."

"Including the twins?" she prompted.

"Including the twins. Especially the twins. I thought—as a former social worker—you might be able to tell me where I go from here to make them legally my kids even if they aren't biologically mine."

Lindsey hadn't had a doubt that this was what Graham would want to do, and yet hearing him say it, knowing it would put him in just the kind of abrupt single parenthood Dave Morrisy had found himself in, tightened a knot in her stomach. "I'll contact some people I know at social services, explain what's gone on. They'll interview everyone involved, do a home study on you, but I can't see there being any problem with you adopting the twins. Their only known parent is deceased, and it's always preferable when that's the case to have a family member willing to take them in."

"So I guess I really am a dad."

The knot tightened a little more. She teased him to hide it. "And a son and a nephew—all at once you have more family than you know what to do with."

"But not more than I'd like to have."

That was a leading statement that Lindsey didn't know how to respond to.

Graham went on, anyway. "I want you to know that I'm willing to give you all the time you need. I swore I wasn't going to rush you or pressure you. But I'm also not going to sit back and let you walk out of my life the

way you walked out of that house this morning. I want you to be a part of my family, too."

A cold shiver of fear ran up her spine at the same time her heart did a leap of joy. And the confusion of those diametrically opposed reactions left her speechless.

Graham pulled their entwined hands to rest on one of his hard, thick thighs and cupped his other hand around them. "I know this all scared you—a whirlwind romance, a man with kids who aren't yours, wanting you to marry me and mother those kids... But there are some differences between what's going on with us and what happened with you and the other guy. Big ones."

"Such as?" she managed in a bare whisper of a voice.

"The kids aren't any more mine than yours. We could adopt them together, as a couple, as husband and wife, for one."

"And for two?"

"I'm not coming from the same position that old what's-his-name was. He was fresh from a tragedy, he was grieving, maybe not thinking straight or clearly, feeling lost, adrift. Not that I'm diminishing his feelings for you. I'm just saying he didn't come to fatherhood or to loving you as freely as I do. To me, having a chance to raise the twins is something joyous. I'm glad to end up with them and I'd like to share it all with you. But it's also something separate from wanting you. I love you so much, sometimes I think I need you around just to breathe or to feel complete, but it doesn't have anything to do with Kate or Charlie. I'd feel this way, I'd want you to marry me, even if the twins disappeared tomorrow."

"That's all well and good, but so much of what you describe in Dave—and it's all true—is happening to me right now," she reminded them both.

He smiled at her. "So you're telling me you do love me but it's probably just a passing thing to get you over the hump of your divorce?" he joked. Or maybe not all of it was a joke.

Still, the way he said it made her laugh. Just enough to ease some of the tension keeping that knot in her stomach. "I don't know, maybe I am telling you that."

"What? That you love me or that you were only using me as your sex slave to heal the wounds of the past?"

His melodramatic rendition made her laugh yet again. "I don't know!" she repeated.

He got serious once more. "You don't know if you love me or not?"

Lindsey pinched her eyes closed, so afraid to admit it out loud. But the feelings were going to have their day no matter what she was worried about, and she heard herself say, "I do love you," in a small, quiet voice.

"I thought so," he said with a swagger in his tone that made her open her eyes to give him a sidelong glance.

"Now who's being cocky?"

"Me." He squeezed her hand. "So how does it feel— loving me? Like a passing fancy?"

"No."

"Good. We're making strides here. Have you contemplated spending the rest of your life with me?"

"No." Not really. How could she have after knowing him such a short time? After what one of life's lessons had taught her about such things?

"Will you think about it?"

He wasn't kidding with that. He was very serious. And now that he'd brought it all up, how could she think about anything else?

But what she said was, "This is crazy."

"I know it. And I wasn't going to approach it so soon. I was going to go on charming the pants off you until you could be more comfortable with the idea that we were meant for each other and that no matter how long or how short a time it took for us to come together, it was still right. But then I turned around this morning and you were gone."

"I didn't drop off the face of the earth. I just left you alone with your newfound family."

"But I started to think that you might drop off the face of the earth. That what had brought us together and kept us together was this case. And now that you'd solved it, you just might slip away from me for good. You might let fear and timetables keep us apart. And I couldn't let that happen. Not without putting up a fight."

He was rubbing the back of her hand with his fingertips in a slow, feather-light caress. Lindsey nodded in that direction. "Is this how you fight?"

"And like this," he said, deserting her hand to cup the side of her face and capture her mouth with his in a kiss that was warm and sweet and so sexy it made something else knot up inside her, though this time it was not unpleasant at all.

In fact it was so terrific she forgot she was in plain view of all of her neighbors, and couldn't resist letting her lips part just as his were or admitting his tongue to dance with hers, or arching against his body when he released her hand altogether and circled his arms around her to pull her close.

Then he ended the kiss to stare down into her eyes with those electric blue ones of his. "Nothing this good is wrong, Lindsey."

"Maybe nothing this good is real."

He frowned at her. "I think it is. But I guess you'll have to be the judge of that for yourself."

He kissed her again, a kiss to knock her socks off even though it didn't last long enough for her to indulge all she might have liked.

"Think about it," he ordered her as he stood. "And when you have, you know where to find me."

Then he turned and left her sitting there on the ledge of her flower box, one glove on, one glove off, and every nerve in her body stretched taut with wanting him back where he'd been before.

But she didn't say that. Or anything else.

Instead she just watched him go, her gaze slipping from those broad, straight shoulders to the narrowing plane of his back to his waist, and on down to hook to the slits of pockets that rode that to-die-for derriere.

Everything about him seemed too good to be real at that moment.

But even as a part of her longed to run after him, to accept his proposal on the spot and drag him inside to prove to him just how much she did love him, a different part of her remembered another time, another man, another child, and how disastrously that had ended for her.

And Lindsey just watched Graham go.

Chapter Ten

Lindsey was set to have dinner with Logan, Quinn and Cara that evening. It was Logan's last day on the police force and the dinner was part commiseration for that, part welcome to Strummel Investigations.

Logan had chosen the place, a family-owned Mexican restaurant called Tafolino's. It was nothing fancy, just a homey, relaxed atmosphere with great food.

Lindsey could see her brothers and soon-to-be-sister-in-law already seated near one of the storefront windows when she pulled into a parking spot just outside the place. As she turned off the engine her gaze focused on Quinn and Cara, and just as she'd experienced when she'd met them all at brunch, she had an initial flash of jealousy to witness them sitting so cozily close together, Quinn's arm around Cara, Cara leaning into his side as if that spot had been specially carved for her.

And somewhere in the back of Lindsey's mind, the voice that suddenly sounded was not that of caution but one whispering that she could have that same thing, with Graham. That same kind of love and closeness....

And, oh, how she wanted it! Wanted him!

She had the urge to turn the car around right that minute, speed to Evergreen and fall into his arms shouting, "Yes! Yes! Yes, I'll marry you!"

But of course she didn't do that.

As much as she wanted to, she was also scared to death to even be considering it. Terrified of the prospect of making the same mistake she'd made before.

So instead she took the key out of the ignition, pasted a smile on her face and went into Tafolino's to join the small group.

"How are you doing?" she asked Logan after greeting everyone.

"Good," he answered as if he meant it. "Of course it helps that I'm headed for Cancun for a week's vacation tomorrow. But still, I feel like a huge weight has been lifted off my shoulders. I must have been more ready than I thought to leave the force behind and go on to new things." And new subjects, because he changed that one to ask what was happening with Graham's case.

Quinn was interested, too, and if Cara wasn't, she pretended to be, so Lindsey brought them all up-to-date.

When she was finished Quinn said, "So you're through with the job and the man?"

Clearly her oldest brother was still worried about her personal involvement with Graham. She considered saying something to make him relax, but then thought that maybe if she talked through her feelings, some of the confusion might be lifted. "The work is finished, yes," she answered, hedging on the other part of the question.

It was Logan who repeated, "And the man," letting her know he was in on the worrying.

"That I'm not sure about," she answered, going on to explain.

But her brothers' concern ran deeper than she'd expected, and the fact that Graham had proposed apparently stirred it up.

"You're on the rebound," Quinn accused, though kindly, compassionately. "Surely you aren't even considering accepting?"

"I'm not on the rebound," Lindsey took issue. "'On the rebound' means a person is looking for a way to bounce back as if nothing happened, to distract themselves and put a bandage on the wound to pretend it's all better when it isn't. I've spent a lot of time tending the wound, dealing with it, analyzing where I went wrong and why. Graham isn't a bandage soothing anything." On the contrary, he was putting her in more turmoil than she'd been in for a while.

"It's so much like before, though, Lindsey," Logan added. "Both men suddenly thrust—unprepared—into single fatherhood, you going to their rescue."

Rescue.

That word set off alarms in her mind. It was the same word she'd used herself in regard to her relationship with Dave.

And yet when she considered it now, with Graham, it didn't fit. And because it didn't fit, it occurred to her that he'd been right when he'd talked about the differences between himself and Dave and their situation.

"The only similarity between Dave and Graham is the sudden fatherhood," she heard herself say. "Dave became a dad in the midst of tragedy, devastating loss, a horrible emotional crisis. I can see now that in a lot of ways he was in orbit, that he needed a safety net to come back down to earth and I was it. You're right, Logan,

it was Lindsey Strummel to the rescue. But Graham is not appealing to those instincts because he doesn't need to be rescued. This is all happening to him at a time when he's emotionally stable and strong, and can deal with it. Plus he's happy about it. He doesn't have to take on raising the twins. He wants to. And he has all the wherewithal and help he needs to do it without me. No, his proposing is for one reason and one reason only—he just wants *me*. Not me-the-wife or me-the-mother, just me.''

And somehow as she said that, she realized she believed it. Not only because he'd told her so, but also because not once had Graham made her feel as if he was attracted to her for any reason but that she was a desirable woman.

''But *you* aren't coming from an emotionally stable place,'' Quinn reiterated, answering her reasoning with just what Lindsey had argued to Graham. ''I'd feel a whole lot better about this if there weren't babies involved again. If it was just that you'd met a good guy and hit it off.''

''You are a sucker for kids, Lindsey,'' Logan added.

Lindsey thought about that while the waitress brought their food. But she had an answer by the time the woman left them to it.

''Kate and Charlie are great. But the same way I believe Graham wants me independent of anything or anyone else, I'd want him with or without those babies.'' And again her own words brought the truth of it home to her. She loved Graham so much it was incredible. Too incredible to have been influenced by the twins one way or the other. Even her own intense reluctance to get involved with them hadn't been able to keep her

away from Graham. Certainly they weren't a part of the attraction the way Bobby had been.

"And as for being emotionally stable," she added, "I admit I might be a little shaky when it comes to romance, but being aware of it has actually made me pretty cautious. And still, this feels right."

"So you have made up your mind," Cara said after staying out of the debate to that point.

It came as a surprise to Lindsey, but it did seem as if she'd somehow arrived at a decision when she least expected to.

Before she could say that, Logan said, "Good grief, you can't be serious. You just met this guy."

Cara laughed and Quinn cleared his throat because they'd had a similar whirlwind courtship and could hardly take Logan's side in that.

Lindsey looked at her oldest brother and his fiancée, at the picture of what she could have, and that cinched it for her.

"As a matter of fact, I think I am serious," she told Logan, never taking her eyes off the happy couple across the table from her. "Because nothing as good as what I've found with Graham is wrong. No matter how fast it happened. Or what came before."

LINDSEY KNEW where to find Graham, all right. But she hadn't expected to come upon what she did when she got to the house in Evergreen.

It was dark by then, and the living room drapes were open, framing an even bigger mess than had been there when they'd arrived from Colorado Springs.

But this time vandalism wasn't the cause.

Kate and Charlie were.

The twins were sitting in the middle of the floor joyously flinging handfuls of dry cereal out of the box to rain down around them and join a package of cookies that looked as if it had been stomped like grapes for wine. Lettuce leaves and fresh cherries smooshed to pulp—not to mention other foodstuffs Lindsey couldn't even recognize—had been torn, thrown or trounced into the carpet-killing mush.

"Oh, you guys," she groaned.

Just then Graham came from down the hallway, seeing the twins and the living room but not Lindsey still standing outside.

His grimace was so extreme it was comical, and she could hear his moan through the screen of the open front door.

Kate and Charlie stopped what they were doing and Kate held a handful of cereal up to him. "Some?"

For a moment Graham just stared down at the little girl, and Lindsey wondered if this antic had stretched his patience to the limit, if he might holler or reprimand or even spank. Or change his mind about really wanting this in his life.

But after a moment he merely accepted the offering, said thank-you and tossed it into the air over the kids' heads like rice at a wedding.

Kate and Charlie shrieked with delight. And Lindsey smiled at the scene, loving him, loving the way he was with those kids, the way he took everything in his stride.

And the rugged beauty of his face, those broad shoulders, that narrow waist, those buns-to-die-for, were all pretty okay, too.

She watched at he tried to get the babies out of the middle of the mess without grinding it into the carpet any worse than it already was. But Kate and Charlie

weren't interested in being moved. They wanted to feed him cereal as if he were a horse that would nibble out of their hands.

And that, too, made Lindsey smile.

Okay, so she did love the kids, too, she admitted to herself.

Somewhere along the way, distance or no distance, she'd fallen for them. But still she didn't have any doubts about the strength of her feelings for Graham, or thoughts that the twins might be the reason she was there at that moment.

No, she loved Graham and she loved the twins. But they were separate from each other, as if all her reminders to Graham to keep in mind that they might not be his kids really had somehow managed to keep her feelings for him and her feelings for Kate and Charlie in different corners of her heart.

And suddenly she just knew that the future would be good. That in no way was she about to repeat the mistakes of the past. For this was not an already-made family in which she was filling a gap. This would be a family she and Graham chose to make from scratch—a man, a woman and two babies, brought together from far corners by fate. She wouldn't be just the substitute mother to children who were, when it came down to brass tacks, only his. These kids would be just as much hers.

And Graham would be hers. Not a man grieving for the loss of another woman and finding solace in her, but a man who just plain loved her.

She knocked on the window through which she was watching them, drawing all three pairs of eyes her way, then three big smiles that told her how glad they all were to see her.

And she had a strong sense that this was where she belonged—with Graham and the twins—that she completed the group as no one else was meant to, and it warmed her to her toes.

Graham ignored the mess, stepping through it without a single glance anywhere but on Lindsey as he made a beeline for the door at the same time she did from outside.

"Isn't this where I came in before—in the middle of a food fight?" she joked as he held open the screen and she stepped into the entryway.

"We just came from the grocery store and I left the bags on the kitchen table while I answered the phone. It didn't occur to me that they could get up there, let alone that they'd drag everything in here and do this—and all in the space of maybe five minutes."

"Oh, you do have some things to learn."

"Did you come to help teach me?" he asked hopefully but warily.

They were still standing in the entranceway, but she angled in the direction of the living room, surveying the mess.

"I'd be out of my mind to take this on," she said, though her tone made it clear that's just what she was there for.

"Do it anyway," he urged. "It's a lot of fun."

"It's a lot of work."

Graham clasped his arms around her waist and turned her to face only him, pulling her close. "I'll do the work. You can just have fun."

"I thought the deal you offered earlier today was for equality. Marriage, adopting Kate and Charlie together..."

Graham grinned down at her, those white teeth blinding her with his pleasure. "That was the deal, wasn't it? And here I am almost letting you off the hook for your share of the downside. What could I be thinking?"

He kissed her, a slow, savoring kiss, as if it were a fresh taste of what he'd been worried he might never really have.

Then he ended it and said, "No rush, no pressure, but did you come here tonight to say you'd marry me, by any chance?"

"That was the intent. That and to tell you how much I love you."

He grinned again for a moment before sobering somewhat. "And all the business about the past and how fast we've happened?"

"Water under the bridge," she said, as if it hadn't been an enormous hurdle for her to go over. "I realized that you were right—there are more differences than similarities between what I was to Dave and what I am to you. And that I love you too much to let fear keep me from what's meant to be, no matter how fast it came about."

He grinned yet again and this time it stuck. "I knew all along you were brilliant."

"No you didn't. You didn't have a clue that this is where I'd be tonight."

"Oh, you're wrong there. That phone call I just took was from Lori Springer. She said she'd convinced Marv to let things drop and that they were going on an extended honeymoon beginning tonight. But when I heard her voice, it occurred to me that I could tell you she'd called to warn me about good old Marv and that I

needed your services as a bodyguard after all. So one way or another, you'd have been here tonight."

"All night?"

"Every minute of it. And of every other night, even if I had to keep making up stories about danger and intrigue to keep you here until I was so deep under your skin you wouldn't be able to leave me behind." His smile now was slow and satisfied. "But this way is much better."

"Mmm," she agreed, accepting another of his kisses.

"You know, you're in for the long haul here," he warned when that one ended. "We're going to get married and adopt these kids and raise them and more of our own together, every step of the way, while we grow old in each other's arms."

Lovely prospect. Except maybe the growing old part.

He kissed her yet again, then said, "I figure one in every two marriages ends in divorce, and you've already had the one, so we're safe. Besides, I love you too much to ever let you go."

"I'm not going anywhere," she assured.

Kate and Charlie had made their way to them by then, and Graham and Lindsey each picked up one of them before Graham wrapped Lindsey in his free arm again and captured her mouth for a full, deep kiss this time.

As she reveled in the feel of his lips against hers, one baby played with her hair, and the other tickled her ear.

And in that moment Lindsey knew that the place she occupied in that group was definitely her own. Carved for her the way she'd thought Cara's place with Quinn was special-made for her soon-to-be-sister-in-law.

Lindsey wasn't standing in any other woman's shoes. She wasn't filling a gap left by anyone else.

She'd finally found her own spot. With a man she loved so much there was no question it was real.

With two kids who had waddled their way into a new corner of her heart.

In a family that was too right to ever go wrong.

Chapter Eleven

With his vacation behind him, Logan felt rested, refreshed and ready to take on the world, as well as his new job. He left his apartment and headed across the yard to the house where he'd grown up, the house that now belonged to Quinn and Cara and also served as the office of Strummel Investigations.

Autumn was in the air and Logan took a deep breath of it. Funny how things worked out, he thought. He'd wanted to be a cop from the time he was a little kid. And he'd tried hard to keep at it even when things had turned sour for him.

But now that that part of his life was actually over, he was really looking forward to doing what he'd become a police officer for in the first place—helping everyday people in trouble—instead of playing watchdog on dignitary and debutante duty, which was what he'd recently been relegated to.

He let himself in the back door, knowing no one was home. Quinn had picked him up at the airport the night before and filled him in on agency business. His brother would be out of the office today on a surveillance. Lindsey was busy moving into Graham's house and planning their wedding and wouldn't be working on

anything for a little while. Logan just needed to settle in and do a few background checks until another case came their way.

He didn't expect that case to come his way within a half hour of settling behind his new desk.

But that's what happened.

And much to his disgust, it happened not in the form of any everyday person, but in the form of just the kind of woman he'd been hoping never to have to cross paths with again.

In fact, it happened in the form of a woman he recognized the moment he set eyes on her when he opened the front door to answer the bell.

Madeline Van Waltonscot.

One of the wealthiest young women in Colorado. The queen of snobs. Snide. Supercilious. Insufferable. In short, one of the biggest witches Logan had ever had the misfortune of watching in action at the society shindigs he'd pulled security duty for.

She was also stunningly beautiful.

Not that it mattered when it was overshadowed by her bad disposition and worse attitude.

She pointed over her shoulder at the sign for the agency. "I need to speak with an investigator, if I could," she said politely.

Politely?

Maybe he'd heard her wrong.

"I'm—"

"I know who you are—Madeline Van Waltonscot," Logan said tersely, leaving her standing on the porch and speaking through the screen in the same tone she'd used on him the single time she'd spoken to him in the past—to demand that he get her chauffeur out of the

men's room and have her car brought immediately, if not sooner.

"I'm sorry," he said in the same way, "Strummel Investigations doesn't do party security, bodyguarding, chauffeuring or shopping accompaniment and package carrying."

Her eyes widened, no doubt at his rudeness. He saw her swallow with some difficulty, as if he'd frightened her, though he couldn't believe that was possible.

"I don't want to hire someone for any of those things you mentioned," she said. "I need an investigation done."

Logan stared at her, wondering what her game was.

But for some reason, as he took this closer look, what he saw seemed softer than anything he'd witnessed of her before, less harsh somehow, certainly more tense, and even—though he couldn't believe it—vulnerable.

Very strange.

But then his encounter with her had been a few years ago, when he'd first joined the force, before a lot of hard work had earned him his way into regular duty.

And eventually circumstances had knocked him back again....

Still, he hadn't had any recent dealings with Madeline Van Waltonscot, so he curbed some of his disdain and gave her the benefit of the doubt.

Somewhat.

He opened the door and invited her in, leading the way to the office, where he took his seat behind the desk, motioning her to the chair in front of it but not waiting for her to sit before he did—just to see what she'd do.

He expected a haughty nose in the air, a dressing down, at the very least a refusal to sit until he stood while she did.

But she merely took the chair, sitting stiffly in it and crossing her legs demurely at the ankles.

"I have to know that what I tell you will be held in the strictest of confidences," she began while Logan was still gawking in disbelief.

"Absolutely," he assured, pulling his gaze from great legs he'd never seen not used to advantage.

"I hope you're an open-minded person," she said, clearly hesitant to say whatever it was she was about to. "This will be very hard for you to believe. Almost impossible, actually. To tell you the truth, I'm having a lot of trouble grasping it myself." She swallowed hard again. "But I'm in the most incredible predicament," she added, as if that was an understatement.

Then she seemed to stall, maybe rethinking whether to go ahead and tell him after all.

Logan watched her, letting silence challenge her to go on.

After another moment she did, though still hesitantly. "I'm not who you think I am. Well, of course I am—on the outside—but not on the inside."

Uh-huh. Sure.

"Have you ever heard the saying 'be careful what you wish because you just might get it'?" she asked.

He arched only an eyebrow at her in answer.

"Well, it seems that that's what's happened to me. Four months ago I was riding in Madeline Van Waltonscot's car—"

"In your car, you mean," he amended.

"Just bear with me." Again the hard swallow. "I was redecorating Ms. Van Waltonscot's guest house. Actu-

ally, I worked for a design firm that she'd hired, and no one liked her, so, being the new kid on the block, I got the job of trying to please her."

"You were working for Madeline Van Waltonscot?" Logan asked dubiously.

"I told you, I'm not who I am."

Oh, good. Lotsa money. Lotsa nuts.

Either oblivious to his growing doubts or ignoring them, she picked up where she'd left off. "Ms. Van Waltonscot insisted I spend an entire day with her—just being her little sponge, she said—so I could get the right feel for her tastes and style. It was a long day, I can tell you. And a long night and into the next morning. She dragged me around until 3:00 a.m., all the while expecting me to be seen and not heard while she talked and talked and talked. A mile a minute. Almost as fast as she drove.

"Anyway, when she was finally taking me home, she gave me this lecture about what she expected from me personally—what she wanted in the way of redecorating, which was more elaborate than anything I'd ever done before, and how much she was willing to spend, which was more than what my entire college education cost. I was riding along, too tired to even care anymore that she was driving thirty miles over the speed limit and only half listening to her by then while my mind wandered. I was wishing I had that kind of money, that kind of life—"

Something clicked in Logan's memory. "Four months ago—didn't I read that Madeline Van Waltonscot had been in a serious car accident that had killed her passenger?"

"I'm sure you did because it's true. Sort of, anyway. What you couldn't have read because no one but me

knows, is that her passenger wasn't exactly killed. Madeline Van Waltonscot was.''

In the pause she let fall then, Logan wasn't sure he understood what she'd just said.

"Technically," she continued, "both the passenger, Maggie Morgan, and the heiress died in the emergency room. But Madeline Van Waltonscot's body was revived. And after three months in a coma, when I woke up...that body was mine." She tugged at her lower lip with teeth too perfect not to be capped. "And not only have I—plain old Maggie Morgan—found myself in someone else's body, in someone else's life...but in someone else's trouble, too...."

THREE BESTSELLING AUTHORS
HEATHER GRAHAM POZZESSERE
THERESA MICHAELS
MERLINE LOVELACE

bring you

THREE HEROES THAT DREAMS ARE MADE OF!

The Highwayman—He knew the honorable thing was to send his captive home, but how could he let the beautiful Lady Kate return to the arms of another man?

The Warrior—Raised to protect his tribe, the fierce Apache warrior had little room in his heart until the gentle Angie showed him the power and strength of love.

The Knight—His years as a mercenary had taught him many skills, but would winning the hand of a spirited young widow prove to be his greatest challenge?

Don't miss these **UNFORGETTABLE RENEGADES!**

Available in August wherever Harlequin books are sold.

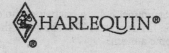HARLEQUIN®

Spend your summer with Strummel Investigations!

STRUMMEL INVESTIGATIONS

American Romance invites you to read Victoria Pade's
Strummel Investigations trilogy! Three top-notch P.I.'s in
the Strummel family—Quinn, Lindsey and Logan—solve
mysteries and find love.

Look for:

#588 THE CASE OF THE BORROWED BRIDE
in June
Quinn Strummel puts his P.I. skills to use when he
looks for a missing groom—and accidently falls for
the bride!

#590 THE CASE OF THE MAYBE BABIES
in July
Lindsey Strummel helps a bachelor who's found twin
infants on his doorstep. Will she solve the mystery—
and become a mom?

#594 THE CASE OF THE ACCIDENTAL HEIRESS
in August
Logan Strummel doesn't exactly believe that his new
client's had an out-of-body experience—but she's sure
got a body *he'd* like to possess!

Strummel Investigations—only from American Romance!

HARLEQUIN®
AMERICAN ◆ ROMANCE®

"Whether you want him for business...or pleasure, for one month or for one night, we have the husband you've been looking for. When circumstances dictate the need for the appearance of a man in your life, call 1-800-HUSBAND for an uncomplicated, uncompromising solution. Call now.
Operators are standing by...."

I ♥ 800
HUSBAND

Pick up the phone—along with five desperate singles—and enter the Harrington Agency, where no one lacks a perfect mate. Only thing is, there's no guarantee this will stay a business arrangement....

For five fun-filled frolics with the mate of your dreams, catch all the 1-800-HUSBAND books:

Coming to you only from American Romance!

HFH-1

FLYAWAY VACATION SWEEPSTAKES!

This month's destination:

Glamorous LAS VEGAS!

Are you the lucky person who will win a free trip to Las Vegas? Think how much fun it would be to visit world-famous casinos... to see star-studded shows...to enjoy round-the-clock action in the city that never sleeps!

The facing page contains two Official Entry Coupons, as does each of the other books you received this shipment. Complete and return all the entry coupons— **the more times you enter, the better your chances of winning!**

Then keep your fingers crossed, because you'll find out by August 15, 1995 if you're the winner! If you are, here's what you'll get:

- Round-trip airfare for two to exciting Las Vegas!
- 4 days/3 nights at a fabulous first-class hotel!
- $500.00 pocket money for meals and entertainment!

Remember: The more times you enter, the better your chances of winning!*

*NO PURCHASE OR OBLIGATION TO CONTINUE BEING A SUBSCRIBER NECESSARY TO ENTER. SEE REVERSE SIDE OF ANY ENTRY COUPON FOR ALTERNATIVE MEANS OF ENTRY.

Dear Reader,

We're thrilled that you're spending your summer with STRUMMEL INVESTIGATIONS. I know you'll agree that this P.I. firm is one unique family business!

Victoria Pade brings us sister Lindsey's story this month. After a three-month hiatus she's got one heck of a doozy for a first case—two beautiful babies and one dynamite daddy!

And don't miss next month's case for an "out of this world" experience!

We hope you enjoy all of the STRUMMEL INVESTIGATIONS trilogy.

Sincerely,

Debra Matteucci
Senior Editor & Editorial Coordinator
Harlequin Books
300 E. 42nd St., 6th Floor
New York, NY 10017

> Maybe... Maybe...she had begun to sound as if she were interrogating Graham rather than just gathering background information.

Maybe her inappropriate thoughts about him had something to do with his evasiveness. Or maybe he just didn't want to answer her. Two could play this game.

"Would you have denied being the father had the mother come to you directly?"

"No," Graham answered readily. "I don't know why *anyone* would leave those babies with me."

Once more she studied him, waiting to see if he would be driven to fill the silence.

But he only stared at her. If there was an ounce of guilt in him it didn't show. And if he wasn't telling her the truth, he was a better liar than any she'd ever encountered.